THE BEAUTY IN
THE BEAST

A TALE OF STOCKHOLM
SYNDROME

C. EDENS

HOLON
PUBLISHING

ISBN: 978-0-9966685-8-3

PUBLISHED BY
HOLON PUBLISHING & CREATIVE COLLECTIVE
WWW.HOLON.CO

Author & Publisher would like to extend tremendous thanks to our Kickstarter backers, without whom this book would not be possible. Thank you, backers, for making sure that this book came to life. We hope you will join us in the future in making more great works come to life.

Contents

In Dedication To:

Kellie Carter
Without you, I would have never found my doctor.
Thank you for everything.

Chapter One

Claudia woke in a panic one morning in her bedroom, a pool of sweat making her skin crawl at the clammy air surrounding her. She gulped as hard as she could as her dry throat constricted and throbbed in pain. Putting a hand to her forehead, she willed herself to calm down.

"A dream..." she mumbled to herself, "just a dream." She didn't know what in particular she had just dreamed of, but she did know it had brought her to such a fright she hadn't woken in a start like that for a very long time. She laid still for a moment, willing her breathing to mellow and her chest to stop vibrating with the fast pace of her heart. When she felt as though she'd good and calmed herself, she hoisted herself to a sitting position.

Around her sat her comfortable bedroom: familiar, tidy. Since the age of four, the room had been decorated with pink furniture. A pink vanity and a pink wire chair sat before her, with pink curtains and a pink bedspread. Even pink bunnies now lay haphazardly across her bed from what she supposed was her thrashing in her sleep. It was like a toddler princess's dream-come-true had puked in her room, and formed all of this frilly, girly mess.

With a scrunch of her nose, Claudia sighed outwardly. Remembering the night before, she realized just how much she needed to move out of her parents' home. As a young adult in college trying to experience life to its fullest, living at home had certainly drowned her plans. For example, the previous night a very attractive man had asked to come in after a splendid date. But she had known better. If the frilly pink of her long outdated bedroom didn't scare him away, her father in the morning certainly would have.

With a long stretch and a yawn, Claudia rubbed the back of her neck tiredly. She felt a little stiff from the lumps in her old, small bed. The morning's aches had become a part of her routine. She had considered asking her parents for a new mattress, or hell, even a new bed altogether. Maybe something a little bigger that she could take with her whenever she decided to move out. Either way, she hoisted herself to her feet to face the day, but not before a nice hot shower, of course.

The post-shower mirror needed a wipe-down with a towel for Claudia to see her reflection. Back at her stared a sparkle-eyed 21-year-old girl. Light, brown hair fell past her shoulders in curls that would tangle in the summertime, frizz into a puff in the spring, and keep her neck warm in the winter. Her lips were round and plump, yet chapped due to an involuntary obsession with constantly chewing them. Her face was clear of blemishes, as she almost never bothered to wear makeup. Besides, she thought to herself, her eyes would just take on an even darker shade of poop brown if she attempted to slather something around them. It was her least favorite quality about herself: her boring brown eyes. Her father had beautiful blue eyes, and she'd wished she'd inherited such gorgeous things. But no, she was met with the cruel fate of boring, common eyes. Her button nose, however, was her favorite feature. It gave her a certain youthful character, something her father always said she would appreciate when she was older.

She slapped her still wet hair into a tiny ponytail as she all but skipped out the door without so much as a hello or goodbye to her parents. She was meeting her friends at their usual morning spot, a locally owned coffee shop, to discuss her wonderful date from the night before. But she also wanted to get there earlier than her friends to enjoy her coffee in a bit of quiet. It wasn't that she was an "introvert" as the kids called it these days, it was just that, occasionally, Claudia enjoyed time to herself. She preferred to avoid the endless chirp of her friends going on and on about her sex life (or lack thereof) as she attempted to wake up with a steaming cuppa. Alright, maybe she *was* a little bit of an introvert. But she was attempting to be less of one. She'd been teaching herself to be more outgoing. That's right; she was much more outgoing than she used to be. After all, she was the one who organized the daily morning coffee runs. She may not always enjoy the squawks of her friends poking and prodding into her life, but she did still enjoy their company. How strange her train of thought was. She chuckled to herself, realizing her justifications were counter-productive. Still, it was a work in progress.

The coffee shop was empty save for a few regulars she recognized from every morning. The carpet looked like it hadn't been vacuumed yet, considering the large breadcrumbs splattered about. They very much clashed with its deep crimson hue. The only thing that could possibly blend in would be the cherry topping from pies, but how often did pies fall on the floor and go unwashed? Claudia's eyes adjusted to the dim lighting of the building. They always kept the shop at a comfortable level of shaded lighting, causing some of the older regulars to even fall asleep in the corners. This morning was no different, as an older gentleman occupied one of the corners, snoozing. Occasionally he'd sniff harder than before, re-adjust, and went right back to snoozing his morning away.

Bookshelves filled with magazines, books, and even DVDs covered the chocolate-colored walls. One end was covered with the day's current newspapers, from the *Times* to the local college paper. She didn't bother reading any of these news reports, but they certainly added to the cozy setting of the small shop. Behind the counter, two televisions sat above coffee machines on both ends, quietly streaming the morning news. The marble countertop glistened from just being wiped down as she approached it.

She didn't even have to make an order as the usual barista, a handsome fellow who she half hoped wouldn't overhear her conversation with her ladies, rung her up without a question. He asked her how her morning was.

"It's going alright. I mean, just woke up and needing that coffee," she said with a smile as she swiped her debit card and tried her best not to look *too* flirtatious. The barista chuckled at her.

"Ya know, these things," he motioned to her coffee in his hand, "are an addiction. You sure you don't come here just to see me?" His eyebrows lifted and lowered playfully. She was reminded of the old cartoons when the hero was trying to pick up the heroine.

"You would like that, wouldn't you?" she laughed back at him, "Why would little ol' me come here *every* morning, spend four dollars on coffee... *Just* to see you?" The barista shook his head with a wide grin on his lips while he poured her drink into a plastic container.

"Who knows? What's that saying?" He leaned on the counter, her order still in his hand, "Insanity is doing the same thing over and over again and expecting different results? I mean, really? Ordering coffee every day, just so you could ask me out." Claudia couldn't hide her smirk even if she tried to. She imagined her face looked like a screwed up mouse.

"Because I'm a girl, and shouldn't have to ask boys out?"

"Not if the guy is at work and shouldn't hit on his customers." His last comment was a literal sing-song as he held her coffee just out of reach. With a wicked chuckle and a lunge over the counter, Claudia's fingers wrapped around the warm coffee cup full of her favorite (plain dark roast coffee, black) and she backed away with a hop and a skip.

"Well..." She bit her lip playfully, reminding herself of the time she'd heard that men found lip biting sexy during conversation, "You'll have to find me after work then, won't you?" Her retort was matched with a giggle before she turned her back to him and skipped to a corner table furthest away from the counter.

Nice, she thought to herself, *played the whole hard-to-get card perfectly. Jesus what a few months of working out and eating better can do...* Claudia had spent her childhood as a plump little thing. No boy had ever so much as attempted to look her direction. Just two years ago she'd started exercising and eating healthier, and the results were beautiful. Claudia felt herself holding her head higher. She had better self-esteem, and felt almost younger. Hell, getting healthier had inspired her "try to be more outgoing" mantra that she was practicing even then. It was as if a weight had been lifted from her body, both figuratively and literally, that she had carried for too long. Don't misunderstand; she didn't have the perfect, bikini toned body. Claudia still perceived herself as average for someone her height. She had a bit of a pudge to her stomach and wide hips that "went for miles" as her friends said, but nothing too noticeable or extraordinary. Nonetheless, she felt doubtful that she could "play the field" without her newly discovered confidence.

She hummed to herself quietly, sipping her coffee and grinning like a Cheshire cat every time she so much as made eye contact with the hunky barista. Claudia noticed it was happening more often than usual. Another glance to the counter and their eyes met, making her blush and grin down into her coffee cup. From the corner of her eye, she could see the barista smile wider and re-wipe the already clean countertop.

This is it, she thought to herself as she tried to cool her cheeks with her hands, *this is the life of an average girl.* She always felt that she missed out on so much due to her weight. Of course, that belief was ridiculous, and she knew it was ridiculous. However, her low self-esteem had never granted her a break from those depressing thoughts. Average sized girls had more catered to them. They enjoyed a better selection in clothing stores, they were never stared at awkwardly in public, and most importantly, others noticed them romantically more regularly.

It wasn't that Claudia thought being bigger would stop her from having an average life. That was ludicrous. It was just that... No. Despite not wanting to admit it, she pretty much believed exactly that, at least for her personal life.

The bell above the door in the coffee house filled the atmosphere with a tiny chime, making Claudia glance up from her thoughts on her body to see one of her two friends that she was waiting for. Becca made eye contact and sauntered over, bringing with her an aura of sexiness that seemed permanently attached to her very being. This girl was the opposite of what Claudia once was; naturally skinny and attractive, she was the whole nine yards. In high school, she had cheered for the football team, while Claudia was stuck cheering for the wrestlers. To some, that wouldn't present much of a difference. To Claudia, it was the difference between those who were popular, and those who wanted to be popular.

Despite their differences in the hierarchy, Becca and Claudia were incredibly close friends. They'd met in camp before their freshman year, and just sort of stuck like glue since.

"Where's Hannah?" Claudia asked as her friend made her way to the table in bright red heels. Claudia caught sight of the hunky barista who, despite having flirted up a storm with her a moment ago, was now ogling her friend's ass in the tight pencil skirt into which she'd managed to squeeze herself. Despite the slight heart-sinking happening inside her chest, she plastered a smile on her lips and looked back to her friend sitting down gracefully in her chair.

Becca was beautiful with every curve, line, and every strand of hair on her body. Claudia figured that even Becca's armpit hair would be beautiful if she had any. The girl dripped of femininity. Becca's blonde hair fell like cascades down her shoulders, shining as though it was spun from pure gold. Her cheeks were always a shade of light pink, her plump lips rosy and wet with gloss. She had dazzling light brown eyes, nothing at all like Claudia's dark ones. Hers looked like caramel, or honey, and Claudia's just looked muddy. If it wasn't a natural glow on this girl, she covered it with a near professional hand at make-up. Cat-eyes, perfectly lined lips, even giving her cheeks a new shape: Becca could do it all in her sleep and look like a million bucks. Claudia could put on concealer and still have lines on her face from not blending it properly.

Becca was taller than Claudia too (by quite a few inches) without the help of heels. And her height was prettily combined with long, creamy legs. They were thin, defined, and simply... Perfect. Claudia wondered if, despite being taller and more muscular, Becca still managed to weigh less than her.

"She's parking. I didn't want to walk far."

"Yeah, I can tell." Claudia chortled as she took another sip of her coffee. "What's with the get-up?"

"Oh?" Becca leaned back in her chair and splayed her pretty pink manicured nails over her lips in a mock shocked look that immediately evolved into an evil looking smirk and a glance around the establishment. "Well... I was hoping to catch the eye of Vince."

"Vince?" Claudia screwed her face up in question. "Who the hell is Vince?"

"Vince. You know." Her friend just stared at her in a you-know-precisely-who-I'm-talking-about way. After a long pause of silence, Claudia merely stared at Becca like a student waiting fo a teacher to answer a question. Becca rolled her eyes melodramatically while slapping her knee in mild frustration. The discomfort was interrupted as Hannah walked in; plain little Hannah. Where Claudia had once been the fat girl and Becca the pretty skinny girl - Hannah was *always* the average one: the one in between. The amazing thing about Hannah though was the fact that it didn't stop her from being the happiest among the three. Where Claudia and Becca were always on the hunt for someone to love (or just "love" for the night), Hannah was already married to her high school sweetheart with plans to start her own little family. Amazingly, she'd managed to stay with him since the seventh grade. Love at first sight, they always say. But Hannah always playfully dismissed it as the two of them settling for one another at an early age.

"Can't get all the boys like you two do, so may as well make sure I always have one to go home to, huh?" she'd joke as Becca would roll her eyes much too dramatically, and Claudia would giggle.

They were cute – Hannah and her husband. But at the same time, Claudia felt they'd moved way too fast. Besides, who commits themselves to *one* person? That would get boring far too quickly. Claudia could see herself as a sort of poly-curious person, someone who would never be able to commit to one person and only one person. So the fact that they'd committed to one another at such a young age and so permanently sometimes scared her. But she'd never admit any of this to her friends. But still... they were cute enough. Hannah especially.

Just as the day Claudia met her, Hannah's hair lay limply on the sides of her head in a simple bob, her face only covered in a basic foundation (that was blended just fine, unlike Claudia's as mentioned before). Her hazel eyes looked tired and a bit annoyed as she slumped into the seat next to Claudia, her broad shoulders drooping to match the sleepiness. While Becca chose form-fitting attire, and Claudia dressed comfortably, Hannah's clothes were baggy, and in no way complimented her body type. To be honest, in all the years Claudia knew her friends, she realized she didn't know *what* kind of body type Hannah had. She'd always hidden it underneath baggy clothing that just gave her a drab vibe. For all Claudia knew, Hannah wasn't plain at all, but a bombshell knockout who just hid it all out of modesty. Nevertheless, Hannah was smart, knew precisely what she wanted, and was a go-getter. Not something Claudia ever was, or even Becca for that matter (besides when it came to men). The other two girls liked to try to play coy and were wishy-washy. Hannah would seize the day and take what she deserved. Claudia and Becca were both a couple of dunces, and in no way knew what they wanted out of life. Hell, Claudia just got a rush from *almost* asking a guy out. That was as close to a go-getter she'd ever come.

"Hannah! Hannah! Claudia doesn't know who Vince is!" Becca was near squealing as Hannah tiredly laid her head on Claudia's shoulder, her hazel eyes staring more past Becca than at her. The signs of a hangover were obvious on her.

"You couldn't be louder, could you? *Jesus...*" Hannah

mumbled more to herself than the company. "And really? You don't know the name of the same guy that serves you your nasty coffee every single morning?" Eyes were on Claudia as she glanced from her friend to the barista who was now looking in their direction.

Shit, was the only thought that went through her head as her face grew beet red and she tried to hide it behind Hannah's head.

"No, it's not! NO IT'S NOT!" she frantically spewed through the hair. Without taking breaths between words, she also managed an "Ohmigodyousaidthatsoloudhe'llknowweweretalkingabouthim!"

It didn't matter. Becca was already cackling complete with her head tilted back, one hand lightly slamming on the table in front of her. Despite her look of distaste in being awake so early, Hannah seemed amused as well.

"Yeah. He's in Hannah's sociology class. God Claudia! You're really spacey sometimes." Becca's voice hadn't lowered from her howl of laughter. Claudia didn't need to look up to know that the barista would be watching them, now hearing himself mentioned multiple times.

"Really? Not knowing my name all this time? Ms. Boswell, I'm almost hurt." She felt her face burn to the point of fire as she heard the voice of none other than the hunky barista right next to their table.

"And you didn't get your usual, Hannah, so here's your mocha latte."

"Thanks," Hannah responded in a mumble as she wiggled her shoulder to free it from Claudia's face. So much for Claudia's strong sense of self-esteem for the morning, it had now been jerked from under her by none other than her best friend. She didn't want to look up at him, but now that Hannah had shaken her from hiding behind the plain bob of hair, she meekly looked back toward the voice.

There he was, hunky barista, standing at their table with a lopsided grin that, to Claudia, could only be described as, "oh-you-so-owe-me-little-missy."

Humiliation couldn't even begin to describe how she felt. Was there a word for more than that? Claudia bitterly thought that she might as well make a word for it, "Claudiaism:" the state of being beyond humiliated.

"I'm so sorry. I guess it must have slipped my mind or...

8

or something…" her hands found a stray napkin as she stammered awkwardly and began folding it into neat little boxes. "I'm sooo sorry." She emphasized the "o" as much as possible, hoping it would show sincerity. It seemed it did, because he seemed pleased with himself.

"Yeah," Becca chided, a mischievous grin playing on her shimmery, plump lips, "She usually just calls you hunky barista." Claudia's face had to be turning from red to purple by now in all of her embarrassment.

"BECCA," she immediately snapped at the woman across from her, staring daggers into her smug face.

"What? We all do. You're just a cutie." Becca's mannerisms in flirting were always at Claudia's expense. It was a quality that was less than Claudia's favorite. For instance, the previous night was supposed to be a triple date with her girlfriends and the boy Becca planned on seeing. But in her better judgment, Claudia prevented it. She didn't need Becca causing one embarrassing incident after another to impress her date.

"Well, thank you, ladies." Vince gave a small nod as the once napping older man woke and called over to him for assistance.

Claudia waited until she knew he'd be out of earshot and much too busy to even try to listen in. When the coast was clear, she straightened her back and glared at Becca hard.

"What was that all about?" She was trying to whisper, but instead it came out as a hiss.

"What?! It's just in good fun. Besides, did you see how much we made his day? He was smiling from ear to ear!" Becca was trying to wave it off as a Good Samaritan deed. Claudia wanted none of it.

"He was smiling before that. Jesus! And you wonder why I never take you on my dates!" Claudia leaned back in her chair and pinched the bridge of her nose. She sensed a headache coming on from not only having to deal with Becca's less than savory mannerisms this early in the morning, but also from all the adrenaline rushes she'd been getting from too much interaction with people. She may have been getting better with her introverted ways, but some days were just too much for her. And generally, Becca would be the one to push her over the edge.

But thank goodness for Hannah, Claudia's constant savior from Becca's wild personality. Where Becca stressed her out,

Hannah was always the one to calm her down, and Hannah was going to defuse the bomb that would have been their argument before the countdown could start.

"Speaking of dates how was yours? What was the guy's name? Matt? He was nice. I liked him." Hannah rubbed Claudia's back to help her calm down. She found a spot right below Claudia's neck that made her entire body deflate. Claudia relaxed against the other woman's touch, and she silently thanked a higher being that she had Hannah around to keep the peace. If Hanna had not found these two at the beginning of their freshman year, Claudia doubted Becca and she would have managed to remain friends. Hannah was the peacekeeper, the mother, and all around the mature one among the three. It was no surprise to Claudia she had so much of her life figured out.

Claudia continued to relax into the neck rubs her friend was giving her, and finally lazily decided to respond.

"Matt was nice. I liked him a lot." Hannah stopped rubbing her neck, making Claudia straighten up and take a sip of her coffee before speaking again. "Smart too. He even brought me flowers."

"That's soooo cute," Becca gushed as she set her drink on the table. She leaned forward to push Claudia to go on. "So... where'd you go?"

"That old Italian place down the street from our bar. It was really good. Wish I could afford to go there more often," Claudia said while tracing her finger around the lid of her coffee.

"Don't we all," Hannah interjected.

"Come on, come oooon," Becca whined like a dog, "get to the good part... Did he take you back to his place?" She was biting her lip in anticipation, fidgeting in her seat as a six-year-old would when promised ice cream. It made Claudia roll her eyes slightly. But in spite of herself, she grinned.

"He lives in a dorm with a roommate-" before she could finish her sentence, Becca was gasping melodramatically.

"Shut UP you did NOT do it with another dude around!" Claudia could feel a blush creep back onto her cheeks as she glanced back to the counter. No sign of Vince. Good.

"No! Nothing like that. He dropped me back off at my place, asked if he could come inside. And..." she hung onto the word for dramatic effect, "I explained since I still live with my over-protective parents it would be a good idea to end the night

10

then." Becca leaned back into her chair as the excitement of the story escaped her.

"Boring." That was all she said in a fake huff, before finishing off her chai.

"So nothing happened? No kiss. Nothing? I mean, I don't often look at other men… but he was pretty cute…" Hannah tried prodding the woman for more information. She somehow knew more was there.

"I mean… yeah, we kissed a bit." Becca's head perked back up like a meerkat.

"A bit?"

"Maybe a bit of making out… but you know." Claudia chuckled in spite of herself. "Jesus are we hearing ourselves? We sound like middle school girls."

"Don't care. Want to know. Is he a good kisser? Oh man, I bet he is!" Becca was close to speaking a million words an hour.

"Becca…" Claudia drawled her name out. "Shush! No one wants to hear about our sexcapades!"

"Hah! The only one getting some on the regular would be Miss I'm-so-boring here. So it's not like they'll get an earful," Becca laughed back loudly. Claudia giggled as it was now Hannah's turn to turn a little pink in the face.

"Our sex life is not up for discussion," she said matter-of-factly as she sipped her mocha. "It's simply not."

"So in other words, you're having *all of the sex*," Becca teased. "Come on. I gotta live vicariously through one of you. You told us like half a year ago you're trying to have kids. What. Is. The. Hold. Up?"

If Claudia lacked in the intelligence department, Becca lacked in attention span. It was typical for their conversations to bounce around like this. However, Claudia didn't mind. It meant their attention was focused on something other than herself for a few seconds.

"Living vicariously? You go home with dudes whenever you want!" Hannah sputtered back before she hid her mouth behind her drink.

"Fine. Maybe I do. But I still like hearing your stories once I get them outta ya." Becca lifted her hands and wiggled her fingers in a sarcastic "I'm going to grope you" fashion. Hannah rolled her eyes; Claudia giggled more. "Your stories are fuuuun. Come on.

Don't leave me hanging." She sounded like a whining child the more she dragged her words.

"There's nothing to tell," Hannah plainly stated, "and that's that."

"Oh, poo on you." Becca stuck her tongue out. "Fine. I didn't wanna picture your husband's dick anyway."

Although Claudia didn't want to, she burst into laughter, so hard that she spilled the remnants of her coffee all over the table. As if he had superpowers, Vince suddenly appeared and began wiping up the mess before it could spill on any of the ladies. Despite his quick reaction, the three girls had already jumped back from their table. The crashes of their chairs to the ground caused a few of the regulars to turn and stare at the four of them.

"Sorry about that…" Claudia said sheepishly as she picked up her chair to sit back down. Vince just gave her a grin.

"It's all right," he said before disappearing into the back. The girls all grew quiet. Claudia glanced over to the televisions behind the counter, where a news reporter was doing a breaking news story.

"Reports of a Bigfoot-like monster stalking our streets at night have become commonplace in our small town of Newsbury. Today some have even begun stating that it's behind the recent disappearances of three of our own citizens." Claudia found herself screwing her face up in amused confusion before calling out, "V-erm.. name.. oh! Vince! Turn up the TV! I need to hear this!" Vince re-appeared from the back with a TV remote. With a few clicks, the TV was loud enough for the three women to listen in curiously.

"Lue-Ann Bouch, twenty-one, was the first of the three disappearances starting six months ago. A homeless man told police that he saw what seemed to be a Bigfoot-like being dragging her away through the cornfield on the south side of town. No reports continued when Charley Shipples, nineteen, disappeared two months later. But with this recent case, a homeless man is once again telling authorities that he witnessed Bigfoot carry away Amanda Lively, twenty-four, two nights ago through the same cornfield." The screen flashed to an image of a scraggly looking man, a beard down to his chest and dirt caked on his face. Their town wasn't the largest; there were only a few homeless people living around. Claudia recognized the man as the guy who occasionally went to her favorite bar for a single beer with the

12

change he managed to scrounge up.

"He was uh... big and hairy. Lots of... Lots of thick... Thick, thick, thick black fur covered his entire body, from his toes on up to his head." The homeless man motioned his hand up and down his body, as if making a point. "He was draggin' the girl while she was screamin'. Screamin', screamin'. I didn't dare get close, lest I get caught by the beast as well. I'm not sure how often we'll be seein' the beast but... But, I definitely don't feel too safe on the streets now. Nope. Not no more."

Across from her, Becca was again rolling in her bigger-than-life laughter.

"It's too damn early for this! Really? It's like a damn ghost story on campus!" Becca was carrying on between her cackles, "Oh man. The junk they run on the early morning news!"

"But that girl, is she really missing? Pity they made her report a laughing stock. Can they actually do that?" Hannah pursed her lips in a worrisome fashion, gliding a single finger over the top of her cup.

"Yeah. I heard about her disappearance yesterday while in class," Claudia responded. "I guess she was in my Chemistry lecture, but not my lab time."

"Dang. That really sucks." Becca responded with a quick frown. "But I mean... Come on. Why would they air this shit? That guy is almost always cracked out whenever I see him. I mean, just *listen* to him!" Claudia nodded slowly in agreement with her loud girlfriend. "To even give this guy some airtime like this is stupid. Good for a laugh, but stupid... Bigfoot? Really? Better watch out tonight guys, or Bigfoot'll getcha," Hannah scoffed in response.

"How many people will be talking about this on campus?" Claudia asked slowly.

"All the morons, clearly," Becca responded.

They were not far from the truth.

Chapter Two

The campus grounds were full of signs, banners, and rallying people. Claudia couldn't believe her eyes. There were the usual freshmen with their guitars on the grass, only now they were singing songs about Bigfoot (to which Claudia wondered, those exist?) Others were passing out pamphlets with information on the creature. There was even a group instructing students to stay safe while out at night, telling them never to travel alone especially when intoxicated. Of course, like any college, there were also extremists who were holding crosses up and walking in a circle, chanting on repeat: free the creature, free ourselves. Claudia noted that they made the least amount of sense.

"How many people are taking this whole Bigfoot thing seriously, again?" Hannah started as the three clambered out of her car to gaze around at the small campus full of people. Signs ranged from "Kill the Beast," "Find The Missing," "Save our Bigfoot," to "Change Our Media." The front of campus was a madhouse. Chanting, screaming, dancing, singing - it was all happening for their cause. And they were everywhere.

Claudia wanted to laugh, but the bizarreness of it all stopped her. She and her girlfriends slowly walked toward the main building of their private college, glancing between one another and the crowd, until they were safe behind closed doors.

"You have *got* to be kidding me," said Becca, her eyes wide as saucers. She glanced at her two friends and Claudia knew that Becca was baffled. "Are you telling me that those monkeys will follow just about anything that they see? I mean for Christ's sake

Bigfoot?! Bigfoot. That's just ridiculous." With an exasperated sigh, she readjusted her backpack on her shoulder. "Anyway, watch out for those people. They are probably the ones you really need to look out for. Not some make-believe creature that is supposedly mucking about." She gave a firm nod to her thought and turned her back. "I'm already late for my seminar. I'll see you guys later."

Without so much as another word, she walked away. Claudia raised her brow and glanced over at Hannah.

"What's with her? She's taking this a little too personally don't you think?"

"Well that's Becca for you," Hannah said while patting Claudia's back, "always thinking everything is the end of the world. Especially when she wasn't the first to be a part of it." It wasn't a mean comment, Claudia knew, just an honest one. Hannah wouldn't purposely say something to speak ill about her friends; she simply knew how they acted. "Don't worry about her too much. I'm sure she'll have forgotten it by lunch. Either way, she's right about the time, I need to get to my class. I'll see you after?" Claudia nodded at her friend as she walked away. However, rather than turning down the hall toward her lecture, she turned back to the door and peered through the window.

She couldn't quite place it, but she'd never seen her town this way before. People came and went, that's how it always had been. But for everyone to be up in arms about three college-aged people disappearing? It was a bit much in her opinion. It's likely they all flunked out, got too embarrassed to face their peers and left without a word. Why would so many people cling to the idea of a magical creature taking everyone away?

To Claudia she had two choices: sit through another dull lecture that would only make her brain buzz with boredom, or continue to check out the insanity going on outside. It wasn't much of a debate. After all, how often did the legend of Bigfoot take over a school? It didn't. She was curious, and she did not believe in the old saying about the cat. As a matter of fact, she wanted to flourish in her curiosity. So with a quick heave of a sigh, she unlatched the door and re-entered the chaos that was the outside of her university.

She searched for familiar faces but quickly found that she couldn't find a single one. The University, although small and private, still had many more people than she was used to dealing with as a self-proclaimed recovering introvert. Nevertheless, this time around, she found herself drawn to all the people, and drawn to the insane story that had captured everyone's attention.

"Did you hear?" A man approached her, barely any taller than she was, with a flyer in his hand. She jumped in surprise at his sudden question and nearly turned away from him until her curiosity urged her to ask further.

"Hear what?" She played dumb as she relaxed her body.

"That it's finally the time of the Messiah. God is raining down and removing the sinners from our very own university. Have you accepted the Lord, Jesus Christ, into your life?"

"Oh erm… Yeah, I did that this morning," she said with a forced smile as she quickly inched away from him. It would seem that curiosity could get her caught in some awkward situations. Before he could go any further, she darted away through the crowd. It was far too early to listen to someone preach to her about religion. She could hear him yell after her something along the lines of "burning" and "not believing the sinners' story about a monster," but she tried to ignore him as she ventured further into the mix of bodies and picket signs.

Finally, before she'd almost given up, she recognized someone.

"Matt!" she called excitedly to her date as she rushed over to his side. His eyes drifted up from the book he'd been clearly pretending to read, met hers, and lit up immediately. Beautiful, light hazel eyes that could keep her entranced for hours.

Although hunky barista was attractive, Matt was out of her league *entirely*. Dark long hair, deep beautiful eyes, and a goatee that gave him a sort of hipster vibe, but she didn't mind it that much. It made him all the more attractive to her. His body was tanned, his hair curled around his ears in waves, and his jaw was chiseled. The glasses on his face only made him look more intelligent.

"Hey, Claudia! Didn't think I'd see you caught up in all of this." His grin was warm, like a summer morning. Claudia had to remind herself not to fall into a puddle of goop at his feet.

"I heard it on the news while I was getting my morning coffee," she said in one breath, giggling in places that shouldn't have giggles. "I mean…" She tried to compose herself. There was nothing more unattractive than a groupie. "It's insane, right?

Bigfoot?"

"Yeah, totally." Matt continued to smile at her, and then scanned the crowd with his eyes. "Saying Bigfoot is ridiculous. And we *really* shouldn't be paying attention to that."

"What should we be paying attention to?" She cocked her head to the side, as he reached for her and wrapped an arm around her shoulders. He led her away from a group of screaming students that was forming to her left. This way they wouldn't have to speak so loudly just to hear one other.

"Well... The disappearances for one. Don't they worry you at all?" Matt glanced down at her, his dazzling eyes laced with worry.

"Not really," she responded with a shrug. She was trying to keep herself composed, making sure she wouldn't blush like an idiot in front of him. Her face had been red in embarrassment one too many times this morning. "Just looks like kids dropping out and not wanting to face the consequences. At least to me it does. Haven't you noticed they're all out-of-state kids anyway?"

"Well, Charley, that guy that went missing about three or four months ago, was my buddy... And he wasn't just going to drop out of college all willy-nilly." His words weren't accusatory, only factual. Claudia inwardly flinched.

"Oh... I didn't know, I'm sorry." Her apology must have gone unheard. "Which makes me wonder- why aren't we so worried about these disappearances? It's baffling, really. Infuriating. I just want to know if my boy is alright." His handsome features drooped when he frowned. As a matter of fact, his entire body was drooping. In the short time she'd come to know him, Claudia had realized that Matt wore his emotions on his sleeve.

"I'm sorry, Matt. Do you know any more information besides... well, this?" Claudia motioned to the crowd; a group of Christian-enthusiasts was getting into a yelling match with a group of people holding signs that said: "Bigfoot is among us!"

"Nothing. His roommate doesn't even know." Matt led her further from the crowd to a little crab apple tree, where he exhaustingly sat down against it. "Sorry for the sudden information. How can things go from great one night to chaotic the next?" In spite of herself, Claudia did a jig inside her head. He thought last night went great too.

"Because people are morons and will follow whatever is

17

the newest thing?" she tried as she sat beside him cross-legged, giving him a smile to help lighten his mood. He smiled back at her, before putting his arm back around her shoulders, and pulling her closer to him.

"Don't you have a lecture right now?" He changed the subject.

"Hmm? Oh... yeah. But I figured this was way more interesting to watch. And if I recall, you're in the same lecture. So don't be nay-saying me." With a poke in the ribs, Matt finally laughed, his beautiful hazel eyes sparkling.

"Right. Right. Who could go to class when this zoo is going on right outside?" He motioned to the crowd with his other arm, toward one of the Bigfoot followers getting in the face of a Christian-enthusiast.

"Ohhh. Looks like trouble," Claudia playfully warned before she whispered into his neck, "Who do you think'll win?"

"If a fight breaks out, I'm just going to laugh. What a ridiculous thing to fight over." He paused for a bit while watching the two get closer and closer to throwing a punch. "I put tonight's dinner on the Bigfoot guy."

Claudia laughed. Despite the darkness of the situation, it felt good to sit with Matt and make fun of it. No matter the situation, it seemed the media could turn anything into a joke.

"So does that mean we're having dinner again?" she purred as she smelled his cologne right behind his ears. She nuzzled his neck lightly with her nose, hearing him hum from beside her.

"If you'll have me, of course. I certainly feel our night was cut a bit too short for my liking... Wouldn't you agree?" He made her feel like the most beautiful girl on campus, bad self-esteem be damned. She gave a flirtatious giggle as she felt his arm wrap tighter around her: down and around her waist.

"Much too short. But then again we have class..."

"And we're learning so damn much right now in that class, aren't we?" He teased her as his face came closer to hers. Matt made Claudia feel dizzy in all the best ways; he was oxygen to her lungs. The very thought of being so close to him made her giddy.

"Mmm... I'm learning a lot. What, you're not?" she mumbled back to him, glancing up into his deep eyes.

Without a response, he kissed her. The feeling made butterflies dance in her stomach and her heart quicken. It was like

18

electricity ran through all her limbs, and her head grew two sizes larger. Every kiss so far had felt better than the one before; this one was no exception.

"I -" Claudia parted to catch her breath, realizing she'd forgotten to breathe. "I could get used to that."

"Could you?" he asked, a wide grin on his face. Claudia nodded dumbly, wanting nothing more than to be kissing him again. But that would have to wait.

The sound of screams interrupted their beautiful little pow-wow. From what Claudia could tell, the first punch had been thrown. A huge fight had erupted right in front of them. People of all shapes and sizes intermingled. Screams pierced the air, punctuated by a flurry of punches and kicks. Claudia motioned to say something, but before she could, Matt had hoisted her to her feet and began leading her away from the mess, toward the dorms.

"This has gone a little far, don't you agree?" he asked back to her, and she nodded quietly, glancing back at the crowd as the fight tore on. She could see someone's fist make direct contact with the gentleman she'd avoided earlier, making her wince in empathy. Sirens were already approaching from the distance. She wanted to chuckle it all off, pretend it was no big deal… But something about this made Claudia feel uncomfortable. Something was looming over her campus, and she couldn't quite put her finger over it (besides, of course, rumors of Chewbacca coming to take over). She chortled softly to herself, enough to push the air from her lungs. As she bit her lip in thought and stole a look back at Matt, her eye caught on something moving about in a nearby cornfield. She stopped the two of them from walking and turned to get a better look.

"Did you see that?" she immediately questioned, squinting her eyes to try to make out what precisely she'd seen. She cocked her head, looking about, all the while tugging on Matt's arm to stop. Ahead of her, Matt stopped, glanced about, and then raised an eyebrow at her.

"See what?" he asked.

"It was… big and tall," she started, stepping now on her tip-toes as though it would help her see. It didn't.

"What, seeing monsters, are you?" Matt gently laughed as he tugged on her hand lightly toward the dorms. "Now, come on. Let's get out of here."

19

She wanted to say more as she thought she saw a tuft of fur poke out from the thick leaves of the cornstalks, but she dismissed it as her imagination being carried away by the commotion. She turned to follow him up and into the dorms.

~ ~ ~

Matt's comforter is more uncomfortable than mine, Claudia couldn't help but think to herself. It was lumpy, and the springs dug into her back, especially when he thrusted. When he rolled off of her, her back was released from a hell made of cotton.

Then again, she hadn't thought that a few seconds prior. Sweat stuck to Claudia's body as she lazily propped herself up on her elbows. They were both out of breath; content, but out of breath.

"Well.. that was... enjoyable," she said through breaths as her chest rose and fell. She heard Matt chuckle as he flashed her a content grin. He groggily got up from the bed and walked toward his shared bathroom. He knocked once, made sure the people from the dorm over weren't in it, and helped himself in to clean off. Claudia took the moment to snuggle further into the uncomfortable mattress and stare at the bunk above her. She felt *good*.

It had been a while since she'd gotten laid. With a roll over onto her stomach, she placed her face into her wrapped arms, a wide smile playing on her lips. If Bigfoot disrupting class got her laid, then so be it. She'd better thank the bastard if she were ever given the chance. A blissful sigh escaped her lips as she closed her eyes and stretched her entire naked body out. She hadn't even heard Matt come back from the bathroom and cuddle up to her quietly. She just felt his skin against hers. Immediately she felt a fire burn between her legs and her belly do flip-flops. Skin touching was all it took for her.

"Mmm round two?" she mumbled into her arms as she motioned to face him. He laughed from the belly, a sound that echoed off the cramped walls of his dorm room. It was low and sexy and full of life. Claudia could record it and listen to it all day, every day.

He took his beautiful arms and wrapped them around her. With a quick hoist, she was on his lap, and he was kissing her once

20

more. Claudia's heart soared. She'd never be able to feel this kind of euphoria ever again.

"Wanna know the crazy part?" he said against her lips. She kissed him more with a simple "mm?" in question from the bottom of her throat. He chuckled and continued to kiss back, and between the kisses she heard,

"That," kiss, "was actuall-" kiss kiss, "ly…" kiss, "my first," kiss kiss kiss, "time."

Claudia felt a jolt of panic run up her spine.

"No *way*!" she suddenly exclaimed, pushing away from his lips and leaning back from him. He kept her in his lap, his arms holding her up so she wouldn't fall backward.

"Well… yeah." It was his turn to look sheepish now. He glanced down at the mattress under them, a small smile tugging on his gorgeous lips.

"Why didn't you tell me?!" she exclaimed, covering her chest with her arms as though she'd been scandalized.

"Well… It never came up in conversation." Matt looked her up and down awkwardly. "Why… Is it that bad that it was my first time? I mean, it's not that big of a deal."

Claudia eyed him warily. Her first time wasn't too large of a deal either: in the back of a car her junior year of high school, with a boy from out of town. Nevertheless, she'd always wished her first time had meant so much more.

"I just… wish you'd told me." She tried covering, although guilt was washing over her.

"Look. I figured I'd tell you cuz.. I think you're really special. I *wanted* to do this with you. Hell, I've been dropping hints since a few weeks ago."

"We've only been on like, three dates," she murmured through biting her lips.

"Yeah, well trying to be sexy during a Chemistry lecture is kinda hard." He poked her in the ribs, flashing a mischievous grin. "Ooh, baby, do you want to combine your O_2 with my C and make CO_2?" Matt screwed his face up to emphasize his sarcasm. "Oh baby, doesn't that get your burner going?"

Claudia was already laughing, the stiffness that had formed in her body washing away as quickly as it had appeared.

"You… horndog!" she managed out between laughs.

"I didn't hear you complaining," he retaliated as he

21

pulled her into a naked hug, his strong arms wrapped around her protectively. "I'm glad it finally happened, though… wait until I tell the guys."

"Excuse me?" She was pushing away from him faster than she had before, an incredulous expression splayed over her face. Like hell, she would be something to brag about.

"I'm joking!" He laughed at her as she glared at him. "Come on, lighten up. Am I really that much of a douchebag?"

Claudia shook her head no.

"Although… double standards. I put ten bucks on you telling your little gaggle of girlfriends the second I'm away."

"I would not!" Claudia tried to look hurt, but his look of knowing he was right made her blush more and look down at her hands.

"Alright, yes. Yes, I would."

"Don't forget to mention how amazing I am, even for a first timer," he said teasingly as he kissed her forehead. She giggled softly and motioned to look up at him, but he'd already managed to capture her lips in another kiss.

Whatever she had with him, it wasn't perfect, but it was damn close. Matt was someone who didn't take things too seriously, and she loved that about him. Did she love him? No. But he was cute, and it was true, he was surprisingly good in the sack for a newbie. Either that or it had been so damn long she forgot what good sex felt like. Still, it was enough to satiate her needs.

"See? So if you get to tell, so do I."

"What is this, a right of passage?" she mumbled against his lips, not knowing if she should respond or just keep on snogging.

"If the passage is your vagina, then yes." Claudia let out an unattractive squawk of laughter as she reached for a pillow and hit him upside the head with it.

"What? It's true!" Matt laughed as she hit him once more.

"My lady parts are *not* a passage!"

"Then… They're the pearly gates of heaven?" he tried. Her face immediately grew beet red. Despite her sudden "closeness" to Matt, she still had her limits.

"Alright, alright. I'm done. I just like teasing you because you're cute when you're embarrassed." He finally let go of her waist, making her flush feel all the hotter as her mouth opened to say something but nothing came out.

22

Finally, all she mustered was a "...*youuuu!*" before she brought herself to hide her face in his chest. Matt laughed more and ran his fingers through her wavy hair.

"See? Adorable."

"Stooop," she play-whined as she curled herself back up on his lap. He laughed a bit longer before a knock came to the door. A quick glance between the two and they were dashing to put their clothes on as if they'd done something wrong and were about to be caught.

"One minute!" called Matt as he struggled with one of his socks. Claudia bit her lip to stop from laughing as he fell on the floor with a loud *thunk.*

His lopsided grin was plastered on his face as he said quietly between the two, "Well, if I didn't look like enough of a jackass..." It earned him another giggle from Claudia.

After their clothes were intact (although barely so, they looked like they'd just been through a tornado), Matt swung the door open to show no one but Becca on the other side. There Claudia's best friend stood, in her skin tight clothes and a shit-eating grin plastered across her glossy, puffy lips.

"Yeah. Thought you'd be here," she said while scrunching her nose in Claudia's direction. "You do realize it's past noon already, right? Some of us from the art department are skipping the rest of the day to start a thirsty Thursday early. You in?" She paused while sizing the two up and down. If it wasn't obvious to her what they were just doing, she was a moron.

"Unless you two are, uh, *busy?*" Her mouth ended slightly open, her tongue tucked under her top front teeth. Her cheeky expression just reeked of knowing what she had just interrupted. Claudia felt mild annoyance toward her friend. She was enjoying this far too much.

"No! Not busy at all!" Claudia's face was, for the millionth time that day alone, beet red. The nerve of Becca! She knew they were busy, and yet she still found it hilarious to embarrass the pants off of Claudia. Claudia noted to bring this up to her when Matt wasn't around.

"Yeah... We're-" Matt trailed his sentence and glanced back at Claudia, who tried to give him a dismissive shrug. She wanted to look aloof to the situation, not embarrassed to hell and back. "We're not. Where are we doing this? The usual bar?" Matt raised his brow with a worried look at Claudia before turning his attention to the woman in the hallway.

"Yeah. One of the guys from my art seminar is bringing Jell-O shots. The barkeep is that one chill dude who will let us bring drinks in so long as we buy more and don't get caught. May as well, right? I mean it's not like it'll kill us." Becca gave a wicked grin as she sized Matt up and down, causing Claudia to shuffle neurotically off of the bed and step in front of him.

"Yeah, that sounds great." Claudia sounded a little too on edge for such a simple question. She didn't like how Becca was looking at Matt, nor how she was acting. Her pompous, teasing ways were more extreme than usual.

"Yeah." Matt smiled warmly down at her, making her fears disappear immediately. One of his large hands softly took hers, and she melted right then and there. "I'm good. Let's go." He made her feel amazing.

He was all she'd ever need.

Chapter Three

Claudia would never be able to tell everyone what had happened to her: how she had been out far too late into the night with Matt, with a bit too much alcohol in her system, or how she got separated from him during a huge street party and began drunkenly fumbling about the streets in order to just get home.

She'd never be able to tell anyone that the beast in the news was real. Within mere seconds, it had managed to run at her, pick her up, and carry her out of the town and through the southern cornfield as though it had been nothing.

Had she really been that easy to take? If she'd been responsible and went home with Hannah that night, nothing would have happened to her. Yet, she felt she had to stay longer and stay close to Matt just another hour or two. It was all just good fun, after all. And Claudia hadn't felt this good in so long. He treated her like a princess, like she was the perfect person. Would she like another drink? Of *course*, she would! He should buy her yet another drink; she could handle it.

She was far too intoxicated to reason with, especially with how she would just keep repeating that she had to stay. *Had* to.

Besides, Claudia didn't live too far from the bars; just a few blocks. She would drink her fill, and if she struck out, she could head back home when she felt the need. She wouldn't talk to strangers, or get into odd cars. She was smarter than that and deserved a night out.

However, when she had attempted her march back to her parents' house, her eyesight was sloshing, and her knees were wobbling. Taking a simple step was more of an inner struggle than a common thing she did day-by-day. The entire world had felt like an amusement ride to her: one she wanted off of. Still, she struggled her way down the street, lost in her drunken thoughts so deeply she was unaware of her surroundings. She didn't bother listening to the grunting coming toward her; she shrugged it off as a nearby couple who'd also had one too many drinks and were now enjoying one another's physical company.

To go at it in public. She didn't want to bother with such a lewd thing. Her face flushed at the thought of it.

Then again... Maybe with Matt she'd consider it...

Before she could give public displays of affection another moment's thought, something had grabbed her *hard*. So hard, as a matter of fact, all the breath was taken out of her, and she was unable to cry out for help. When she finally gained her composure and let out a scream, she had realized it was far too late. They were already out of the town. The sudden alarm had sobered her just enough to comprehend her predicament; she desperately began to flail as hard as she could. The thing, whatever it was, only had hold of her waist over its shoulder, so flailing her legs and arms was all she could manage. She flailed this way and that, occasionally kicking and hitting the back and face of this being. The punches didn't faze it. It just continued to run, only grunting in response to her struggles. While she failed to notice at first, she could finally tell that the grunts weren't human. The creature's grunts sounded like the snorts of an animal. And all her blows came down on thick, matted fur.

The drunken homeless man was right. Bigfoot was abducting college students.

It was running on its hind legs, but it looked as though it shouldn't be. Haunches bent back like those of a canine, covered in black fur splotched with burned skin. It looked almost as though it was having difficulty staying upright as it continued to huff and growl while it made its way to wherever it was taking her. She continued to kick and hit it while her broken mind tried to make out what was going on.

During some moments, she mused that she was just having a nightmare. She'd listened to too many news reports about

26

a supposed Bigfoot whisking away college kids in the night, which was beyond silly. There was no such thing as Bigfoot, or any other monster for that matter. Perhaps she was dreaming?

Yes, she had to be dreaming. She was actually in her bed right now, snuggled up under her warm blankets. She would wake up and tell her friends the bizarre dream she had thanks to these stupid reports.

However, when a claw pierced her skin to re-adjust its hold on her, the pain was enough proof to her that she wasn't about to start waking up. Somehow, this was happening to her.

Thick, dark fur covered the thing, with some bald spots revealing charred skin. Its head seemed unnaturally long, punctuated with two ears on top, although one ear flopped to the side as though it wasn't correctly attached. A closer look revealed that the lopping ear was held together by mere stitches from a sewing needle and thread. It had teeth, long and sharp, and dark, black eyes that never so much as bothered to look down at her.

By morning, the creature had slowed down and was now showing extreme distaste for walking on its hind legs. It had finally let Claudia down, with a warning snarl at her. Despite its warning, the now sobering Claudia decided to make a break for it. Before she could get so much as a foot away, the animal bounded in front of her, now on all fours, growling with a ferocious face. The petrified girl squealed in fear as she covered her face with her hands and hunkered down to the fetal position, shaking harder than she ever had before.

From what she thought would be a monster getting ready to eat her, came a long pause of silence. She finally mustered the courage to uncover her eyes and look to see what was happening. Before her, on all fours, stood the creature. With a good look she realized that rather than looking like Bigfoot, it looked much more like a dog; a deformed dog, but a dog nonetheless. The floppy ear hung limply to its head; Claudia could see the sewing string stretching at the weight, crusty and showing signs of being very old. Its eyes were dull, its teeth much too large for its mouth. There were patches around its body where fur no longer grew, along with its tail, which had no fur at all. Its paws, or what should have been paws, seemed to be larger than her head, and had awkward looking *human* opposable thumbs on each one. It was as if someone had decided to add the thumbs on it as an afterthought. Due to the

27

hasty add-on, neither seemed to work. They both hung loosely, just as its limp ear did, on their sides. The creature was both terrifying and pitiful in its state. But with a growl coming from deep within its throat, and its maw snapping at her every time she tried to walk away from it, Claudia decided to follow it toward wherever it was taking her while her mind buzzed with a way to escape.

By the afternoon (or was it the afternoon? Claudia had lost time in her mind, and the sun had passed the middle of the sky so long ago) they approached a field full of dead corn. The poor vegetation was black and wilting, giving Claudia a feeling of bleakness. Her throat tightened as she glanced at the creature, which was now staring at her without moving.

Was it now going to eat her? Was she a dead woman? No one would find her body out here, at least not for some time. Then again, if it ate her, what would it leave behind? She didn't see any decomposing bodies around, so she had to suppose it ate the entire body, bones and all. The idea that her family and friends would never see her body again, never getting that closure, caused her eyes to water up.

The animal nudged her with its head, toward the corn. She looked at it, confused. Its only reply was to nudge her toward the corn again, then grab the bottom of her shirt with its mouth. It began to drag her through the field. Was it trying to make sure she wouldn't get lost? Her mind boggled. What exactly was the meaning of this abduction? It surely was going to eat her, because otherwise why care if she got lost?

Suddenly, from the clear sky, she heard it for the first time. At first, she told herself it was her imagination, but then she heard it again. It was shrill, almost manic. Her heart soared, the sound was clearly human! They were already on her tail! She'd be put into an ambulance any second now and taken home to tell this terrifying story to her family and friends.

The laugh sounded like that of a woman, shrill and shrieking, and she didn't bother to ask herself why her rescuers were laughing so madly. She found herself walking toward the laugh, faster and faster, until she heard her shirt rip and she realized that she was running with the creature right behind her, letting out what should have been the bark of a dog. The laughter continued, on and on, becoming more and more shrill as she came closer. Her ears were burning with the sound, her heart racing because of her excitement of being rescued already and out of fear of the animal behind her.

She came to a clearing, and this clearing made her heart immediately drop, her stomach threatening to lose what little contents it had. There were no rescuers - only a little cabin occupied the clearing. This cabin was old and in some sections falling apart. She could see duct tape filling some of the holes, albeit barely. On the porch of this little cabin stood a single person, their back turned to her with a black, hooded sweater covering their appearance. She licked her dry lips and glanced down at the animal, which had stopped at her side curiously.

What a fool she was. The animal had been bringing her here the entire time. She felt a bitter hatred for the thing beside her as it nudged her toward the cabin. Her legs began carrying her, slowly and carefully. It was then that she realized the shrill laughter was coming from the person standing with their back to her. There was no one else.

"Excuse me..." her voice cracked and her throat burned. She had been screaming for a majority of the night, and it hurt to speak.

The figure now turned and removed the hood, revealing the head of a strange looking man. For first impressions, he looked incredibly strange. Nothing about him matched, especially age-wise. His speckled gray hair reminded Claudia of her father, who was well into his 50's by now, but his face looked so young she dared to say he was barely even legal age. The most prominent feature about him was his eyes: bright blue and cold to the glare. One pupil was significantly larger than the other, giving the impression of a man long gone mad or on drugs. He was only a few inches taller than her, as she realized when she walked up onto the porch. A hand reached out to her asking her to shake it, and she examined it closely. The palms were large, and his fingers were long and spindly. His knuckles seemed almost too small for his fingers, causing quite the straight line if he pointed them directly. His gaze was unwavering, examining her as his hand remained outstretched toward her.

Reluctantly, she slowly took his hand and shook it. His touch was freezing, as if no blood ran through his veins. She shivered. When the very quick handshaking was over, he took his hand away as if it'd been burned by her. He cradled his hand with the other, still watching her intently.

For just a moment, there was calm. Claudia began to wonder if this was all just one huge joke planned by her friends. But to go this far was a bit much.

"Come, come," he beckoned, his voice far more high-pitched than that of a grown man, reminding her of nails grinding on a chalkboard. Then, a realization hit her: it had been him laughing maniacally all along.

Slowly, she followed him into the cabin, and she immediately noticed that it stank of what she could only describe as death. Her initial reaction was to turn and run, but she knew if she did that, that dog-thing would bog her down and take all the life left in her.

The door closed shut, diminishing all the light in the small building save for the fireplace in the far left of the cabin. The man before her turned again, eyeing her intensely. A long silence hung between the two of them. Finally, he grabbed her by the wrist and dragged her away from the fireplace, further into the dark.

Claudia had always thought that if someone were to kidnap her, she'd fight back. But now, in this predicament, she felt limp and terrified. She let this man drag her through the cabin to a far back room. Trinkets and whatsits littered the space. She spotted saws stained in red, pinchers, thermometers, and things one would only see in an old-timey room of a mad scientist.

The man led her to a table in the middle of the room and motioned for her to lie on it. She obliged, too terrified to command her body to do anything but listen to him.

The man watched her curiously as she laid herself on the table, one spindly finger tapping the bottom of his pale lips. His eyebrows, one white and one brown, furrowed in thought. He was silent.

Finally, he grabbed a metal chair from one side of the room and dragged it over to her left side. He sat upon it and stared at her for a long while.

Claudia didn't say a word. She could feel her entire body screaming at her to do something, but in this predicament, she felt too much fear to do anything. The saying "scared stiff" rang true in her predicament.

When he spoke, it stung her ears.

"Why you no leave? No screaming, no struggling, just

listening." When she glanced at the madman sitting next to her head, she could see nothing but curiosity lighting his cold eyes up. She swallowed hard, her throat feeling like sandpaper. She parted her lips just slightly, and tried to speak, but found she couldn't even do that. Her body had betrayed her. She was now in the hands of this man.

"Doctor Cornelious I is, at your service," he quipped at her with a grin. "And you've met Schnuggles. Sure you've spent quantity time with him! Or is it quality? Either way!" Dr. Cornelious tilted his head at her in thought. For a moment, she thought he was going to reach for a horrible tool to begin taking her apart, but instead, all he did was poke her in the cheek with one of his spindly fingers. The curiosity in his eyes was obvious to anyone who could see them, and it grew more and more by the second. The young face of the man lit up, questions passing by silently, eyebrows raising and lowering in thought.

Claudia could hear the animal come into the room. She could only bring her eyes down to look at it. The animal rested its head on its master's lap, its naked tail wagging happily.

"What's that, Schnuggles?" the doctor asked in his cracking voice. The creature looked up at Claudia and jumped to rest its front freak-paws on the table. She could see the thumbs flop to the side and land with a small clunk on the table. A shudder ran through her spine as she wondered if this dog-thing's thumbs were once attached to some of the other victims reported on the news.

The creature licked Claudia square on the face, and she could feel a terrified shudder escape her wavering lips. It then continued to make what should have been a bark, then turned to look at the doctor with a wagging tail.

"Alright! Well… time for an experiment!" the doctor exclaimed. The creature responded with a low growl, not too menacing, but enough to speak to its master.

"Oh, what? You always want to keep one. Just because YOU chose her doesn't mean she's yours." The doctor was standing now, walking over to one of his saws. The dog-thing, standing its ground, growled once more, this time more sternly.

"You are NOT keeping her. If you really wanted one why not grab a boy? A YOUNG one at that. How old is she? Why do you want a milkmaid?" The lunatic was having a conversation with an animal. Once more, the dog made a final unheard argument to

Claudia's ears, causing the doctor to throw a miniature fit, complete with stomping feet and balled up fists.

"Fine. But you don't get to keep ANY of the others. You get this one and this one ONLY." The last word was so shrill to her ears; she thought her eardrums would burst. The doctor bustled like a child being sent to his room, a huge slam of the door following behind him, leaving the dog-thing and Claudia alone.

She was puzzled, to say the least, as to what the hell had just happened. The dog now took its front what-should-be-paws and laid its head on the table. At that moment, the creature did look just like a dog and nothing more, as its doe eyes looked up at her waiting for a pat.

Claudia listened for some time, but heard nothing. With her body crying to let herself just lie there a bit longer, she raised herself on her elbows and stared down at the dirty floor beneath her feet. She sat with her legs swinging over the side of the gurney until she could finally will her legs to bring herself to stand. The creature, Schnuggles, gave a snort at her, having never moved from its spot next to her. She cringed at it. Why had this thing brought her here? It clearly hadn't spoken a word to the doctor, and yet supposedly it had also saved her life.

She didn't have time to doubt the creature's ability to communicate, as she felt the first of many tears rise to her eyes and cloud her vision. The reality of the situation hit her so hard she felt her knees buckle, and she found herself crumpling to the dirty floor with the dog-monster sniffing at her while making what seemed to be whimpering noises.

She was just kidnapped. She was somewhere far away from home and had no idea which way to go to get back. Then again, could she go back? The man had mentioned "keeping" one. Did that mean they intended to keep her there?

A sob escaped her throat as a shaking hand covered her mouth in fear of losing what remained in her stomach. It echoed off of the empty walls and fell back to her ears. Her body began to tremble with such ferocity that her breathing grew more difficult. In the back of her head, she heard the man's words over and over.

They were going to keep her.

They were going to keep her.

Chapter Four

She found herself stumbling out of the pseudo-hospital looking room and into a hallway, tears still blinding her and her body shaking so badly that she felt like she was on vibrate. Although Claudia was attempting to keep quiet, she found herself falling into the walls in the dark, and kicking every nook that could exist. She kept a hand over her mouth the entire time, attempting to muffle any noise that might escape. Despite her efforts, occasional muffled yelps escaped from her.

She didn't see the man, but in the darkness she doubted she could see anything. In the back of her mind, she wondered if it truly was so dark in this hallway, or if she was going into such frenzy that her mind was playing tricks on her. She tried to will herself to calm down, but her efforts merely caused more panic. Claudia hit a wall, realizing she'd gone the wrong way down the hallway and was heading deeper into the cottage. Without her want, both hands came to catch herself against the wall and a loud yelp escaped her. The sound echoed off the walls until disappearing into the darkness. She stood in the silence, waiting, listening.

Nothing. Not even the patter of the paws of that thing on the floor.

Before she could comprehend the sudden strength that had taken over her, she was bolting in the opposite direction of the wall. She saw a light ahead - why hadn't she gone that way before?

Bursting into the dimly lit room (how long had she stayed in that room?) she found herself in a crowded and dainty kitchen. She stood at the edge of the kitchen, and beyond an L-shaped counter was a living room - all the walls layered in books and papers. Only two pieces of furniture sat inside the room - a lush red armchair and a moldy looking, unused couch. The smell of mildew filled her nostrils as she frantically glanced about the area. To her left was a small dining table, beyond it between what separated the kitchen and living room - a door that seemed to lead outside.

Without another glance she darted for the door, her mind no longer giving orders as she solely reacted on fight-or-flight. But before she could twist the knob that somehow appeared in her hand, she felt them.

The hands. They were on her shoulders. They were strong and spindly, and suddenly Claudia smelled something she hadn't quite noticed before.

Peppermint.

The smell was nearly bittersweet, both relaxing and queer as her body tensed up in realization she'd been caught trying to escape. Then again, was she surprised? In retrospect, she was banging around the entire building complete with yelps and sobs. She hadn't necessarily made this a sneaky escape.

"Are we going somewhere…?" From behind her, she could hear him. That high-pitched voice, the one that unsettled her and sounded more female than male. It reminded her of a bird of prey was squawking over its meal before making the final blow.

She swallowed back a sob, resisting the urge to turn around. Instead, she merely stood with her hand still on the doorknob. The smell of peppermint grew stronger as she felt the tickle of hair against her cheek.

He'd leaned over her shoulder now, their faces right next to one another.

"Not a day to go anywhere, no it's not." Even his whisper sounded like nails to a chalkboard. "Not a day. Not a day." His grip on her shoulders tightened as he pulled her away from the door. Her hand wouldn't let go. Tears freshly fell from her face as she realized the second she let go of this door, it would be the moment she gave up escaping.

He tugged her shoulders for a moment, a disgruntled sound coming from his throat. Finally, with a glance to her hands, he wedged himself between her and the door, and calmly, almost delicately, peeled back her fingers one by one.

But it wasn't enough to simply peel them away from the

knob. No. This man peeled her fingers as far back as they would go. The first two popped uncomfortably, causing Claudia to let out quick yips of pain. The yips would make him move on to the next. But the third finger, he just kept going, pushing the finger further and further until finally Claudia had to let go to avoid causing actual damage to it rather than mere discomfort.

The man stared at her with a smug smile playing his lips.

"There we go. Many easier!" he said happily as though he hadn't just tried to break one of her fingers. He reached into the pocket of his scrubs and retrieved a handkerchief, wiping his hands vigorously as though he had just touched the vilest thing in existence.

She stood still, not knowing precisely what to do to avoid more interaction with him.

"What you doing? Don't stand there looking dumb," he suddenly quipped as though speaking to a friend. "Go and sit on the couch or something. Not a day to go anywhere!" He looked exhausted as he helped himself to the armchair and lowered himself on it clumsily. Claudia continued to stand, staring.

"Come, come!" he snapped again, "sit!"

She moved as though on autopilot, one leg in front of the other. Before she could fully fathom what she was doing, the disgusting old couch had enveloped her. Immediately the smell of mildew hung to her nose, which made her eyes water. Suddenly, the dog-monster bounded over and hoisted itself onto the couch, draping itself across her body.

She tensed. Her entire body felt as though she was suffering from rigor mortis. To her left, the man began going over notes and mumbling to himself. The monster simply stretched out, much like a dog would, and fell asleep.

If Claudia could have screamed, she would have.

~~~

Dunce girl. He had given her that name very early on in their interactions. It wasn't a very imaginative name, but it was something that seemed to keep the doctor amused.

"So when are you going to speak? You can speak, yes?" He was standing in the connected kitchen of the small cottage, cutting an onion, behaving as if they were two of the most casual acquaintances. He glanced her way, shooting that icy glare her direction. Every time Claudia so much as saw a hint of his eyes, she would flinch. She could feel them pierce her skin, feel them seeing right through her, causing her entire body to stiffen and ache. However, she preferred him looking *at* her rather than looking her directly in the eye. Eye contact was *painful*. It made her eyes twitch and water up, almost as if they were trying to force themselves from her head. If she weren't scared of making noises around him, she would make pained noises every time she was forced to make eye contact with her captor.

Claudia found herself staring down at the empty plate in front of her. It was one of the few times she had moved from the couch since she'd first sat on it. Even now her palms sweated from being away from the one place she'd associated with feeling safe. Her entire body was quivering, her mind screaming at her to find a means to escape, but she was completely hopeless at that moment. Her body was shaking uncontrollably from the loss of food, water, and rest, her mind breaking at the thought of escaping.

"No speaky? Yes, speaky? You forget how?" The doctor continued to babble on and on. For the past few days, he'd been warming up to her, although she would respond by becoming more distant. During the first few days of her capture, he ignored her existence… But now, he was trying to cook for the two of them while starting small talk.

Her lips pursed together as she glanced from her empty plate to the doctor. Schnuggles was gone, and had been since that morning, probably off to grab more city folk. A burning sensation grew behind her eyes at the thought of another person being dragged here to do whatever it was the doctor did in that terrifying room with the table. She forced back tears from the thought as a small squeak forced its way up her throat.

The doctor's head perked.

"A-hah! So you can talk!" the doctor exclaimed to her. "I knew it, yes I did!" He was now chopping carrots, the onions dumped into a big pot that had bubbling food inside of it. "Tell you what, tell me your name and you get two helpings of stew instead of one!" he squeaked happily. He was grinning ear-to-ear, his pale skin glowing in the moonlight that shone through the window.

Despite her efforts to keep quiet, the idea of two helpings of food made Claudia's stomach growl quite loudly. She doubled over to try to silence the sound, but to no avail.

"We'll start small…" the doctor offered to her as he finished off the carrots. "What's your name?" Without trying, Claudia's gaze came back up to the lithe figure of the doctor. She stared at him, long and hard, but avoiding his eye contact. Her voice scratched at her as her mouth dropped open.

"Claud…ia," she breathed quietly, body tensing and wincing as the doctor moved toward her with a hand to his ear.

"CLOD? Your name is CLOD?" She stared at the doctor dumbly, wondering if she should correct him or not.

"Forgot your own name? My my, you really are a dunce, or as you say, CLOD." The doctor bit the word "clod," letting his teeth snap back together at the "d" in a sickening chomp. "You know what? I'm calling you Dunce-girl. Only a dunce would mistake their own name for clod. Dunce-girl." The doctor continued to cackle to himself as he tended back to the supper. "So, Dunce-girl, do you like carrots?"

"What?"

"Car-rots! CARROTS! You more dunce than I thought!" He looked at her with an exasperated sigh. "Well, you eat carrots. They good for you! And you look worse for wear." He scooped some of the stew into his ladle and took a sip. It seemed to please him, for he continued to scoop more of it into a bowl and forced it in front of the girl.

"Why would you care for my well-being?" Claudia questioned quietly as she glanced from the soup to the doctor, feeling like a mouse sniffing the cheese on a trap being watched by a hungry cat. She scrunched lower into her seat as the doctor looked back at her, and approached her slowly. He came closer and closer until he was eye-to-eye with her, and she could smell the queer smell of peppermint.

"May as well keep you well kept while you're here. If you're sick or weak, you're nothing but a burden to me." He spoke those malicious words in such a sing-song attitude it made Claudia feel sick. "Don't worry. It's not poisoned. Schnuggles would be angry if I just killed you off. Besides, I'm no murderer! I'm a scientist!" He moved away from her to make his bowl.

The girl sat like that for a bit, staring wide-eyed at the madman. It wasn't until she watched him finish his food and disappear off into the darkness of the cabin that she even touched her now-cold food.

Surprisingly, it was delicious.

~ ~ ~

How long had it been? Two months? Two days? Surely it hadn't been over a year... or had it?

The light peaked through the cracks between the planks on the windows as she stared blankly, pondering to herself. Her head rested against the seat cushions of the couch while her legs were propped up onto the backrest. It was comfortable lying this way; it stopped the light from blinding her as much. When the rays of light poked through the wood just right, it would hit her eyes directly. The light stung her eyes, for she'd stayed in this cabin for so long she couldn't even begin to guess how long it'd been.

She lazily placed one hand on her forehead to shade her tired eyes. Although it stung, she welcomed this pain that proved to her that she was at least still alive, if one could call it that.

She lay like that, on the dusty couch that reeked of mold and mildew, unmoving for as long as she could. Not moving meant no communication. No communication meant no pain. And no pain meant another day she could live.

The light continued to flicker through the planks, and she twitched her fingers to play with the streams of light. In her mind, she pictured the light as water, her twitching fingers weaving bags to catch the water. The more water she caught, the more life she could save. She twitched, weaved, and filled her imaginary bags using as little energy as possible, her tired eyes aching and begging for her to look away into the dark. But the dark was a desert, and she needed to fill herself with more water before she wrenched back into the darkness.

Her fingers continued to twitch and twirl idly, her invisible bag catching water with imaginary vigor. With a quiet sigh, her head fell backward until she felt the top of her head touch the hardwood floors. She could feel the thumps of something a few feet away, and she could only guess it was that thing she heard the madman constantly call Schnuggles. What was so "snuggly" of that decrepit creature? Its arms were thicker than those of any football player she'd ever seen, and its head bigger than any cow's. It was repulsing to look at, yet her captor dared to call it snuggly like it was a cute little puppy dog.

Thump, thump, thump.

Just another reminder that no matter how much imaginary water she caught, it would always stay that… imaginary. Nothing was going to get her out of this place. Nothing would bring her life.

Thump, thump, thump.

She closed her sore eyes and swallowed as hard as she could. A bulge that had been growing in the back of her throat threatened to choke her. She could tell by the thumps that it was growing closer, and her body stiffened. Before she could move, she felt something looming above her dangling head, and heard the sniffs.

The sniffs sounded like a dog inspecting something, a few short and quick inhales with one final exhale. The sniffing accompanied a wet, slimy nose pressed against her right ear, sending shivers of panic down her spine. Her eyes clamped together more; her fingers stopped moving.

It sat and sniffed her for a bit until it finally grew bored of her and took a few steps away to thump down on the floor. She waited, knowing the monster was near her, until she slowly opened her eyes to see where it had taken its place of rest.

What she saw was something unexpected, and made her nearly fall off the couch altogether, but she caught her composure just in time. At first, she'd thought a decapitated head had been placed right in front of her own. Instead, it was that of the madman himself, staring intently at her.

The dullness of his eyes had deceived her, leading her to mistake the man's head for that of a corpse. The only emotion she could see in those eyes was an empty curiosity; beyond that, nothing. It was as though all other emotion had been swiped from his very being. All that remained of him was the empty carcass that ate, slept, and did horrible experiments day in and day out.

"Good morning, Dunce-girl." His chalkboard-screeching squeal was raspy. He hadn't been talking much this day. "Sleep good, yes?"

Claudia fidgeted, uncomfortable that her captor was so close to her face, until finally she was able to roll to the side and away from him in one quick swoop. She bit her bottom lip nervously as she glanced back at the boarded windows. No light shone through them now, and she'd lost her imaginary water of life in her panic.

A sweeping feeling of dread fell over her body as the harsh realization that she was still stuck there hit her once more... How long HAD she been here?

"I told you... that's not my name," she finally murmured with care as she watched the mad scientist saunter to his armchair. He chuckled to himself loudly as she responded, legs in the air, wiggling like he was some four-year-old during a comedic children's movie.

"But, you are!" he retorted. A grin capable of putting the Cheshire cat to shame snaked its way across his face, exposing his glinting pearly whites. His head tilted slightly to the side as he grinned and stared at Claudia as if she was yet another experiment to be had. It sent more panicked chills down her spine. She could feel her palms grow cold and clammy as ideas of what he might want to do to her filled her mind. Would he rape her? Do horrible experiments like she'd heard from the other room? Or would he just kill her now and have pity on her?

She watched those piercing blue eyes stare at her, almost without a blink, until her psyche couldn't take it anymore and she found herself looking away, into the darkness of the cottage.

"You said your name was CLOD. Like the dunce you are, Dunce-girl!" Dr. Cornelious piped up again, his manic smile never leaving his lips. "I prefer Dunce-girl much more. Almost pet name like, you see?" He was acting like he was having an average conversation with someone on a Saturday night.

Nothing would ever be average about this man. He'd continue to prey on the innocent, subjecting them to heinous things for the sake of his twisted ideals of "science." He would never have an average day, wouldn't carry out an average life, and sure as hell wouldn't have an average conversation with someone. Especially someone like Claudia after taking her hostage for god knows how long.

Slowly, Claudia pulled her aching legs up to her chest. Was her body always this achy? When had it started? And why now? She continued watching the darkness, but she knew those damn eyes were still staring at her with that grin. That shit-eating grin. How she was learning to hate it.

"Dunce-girl. Are you listening?" From the corner of her eye, she could see his head tilt to the other side. She licked her chapped lips and felt a minor sting to it. Without looking away, she responded.

"Yes." Her answer was quiet and short. How many nights had he tried this now? God, how could she even try to keep count? It was the same every night. She'd wake up and try to stay still, but he would eventually figure out that she was awake and talk to her. The conversations would always stay the same. He would talk in her direction, and she'd only respond when it seemed necessary.

"Good!" he squawked contentedly. One of his grasshopper legs had folded up on the other. Both his hands rested on his knees. He looked comfortable.

"Today's experiment was another fluke. They always scream... So many screams..." The doctor paused in what seemed to be his outward thoughts, "Methinks the screams keeps me from getting more answers. That or life expectancy. They die much too quickly! Much much!" One of his hands came up to his pale face, and his spindly fingers rubbed on his chin.

Claudia glanced his direction, her stomach flip-flopping. Would he share gruesome details of his last victim like he did the other night? It had left her sickened and sleepless until she passed out. At times, she'd replay the words in her head without trying, and feel her knees buckle.

"What can I be doing wrong?" he said, breaking through her thoughts. Through the shadows of the cottage, all Claudia could see was his single brown brow furrowed in thought. She had to look harder to see the white one. How he'd managed to achieve different colored eyebrows still baffled her, but then again, this entire situation seemed like something out of a horror book. A mad scientist capturing a girl in his cottage in an old, abandoned corn field while he experimented on the people of her town wasn't something incredibly believable for the real world.

Not even his hair was very believable. Some of the hairs almost seemed alive, bustling with life, while the rest lay dead, admitting their defeat. The white strands would always fall in his face, sometimes covering those menacing eyes, while the brown would stick this way and that, like horns. Picturing the doctor as a devil wasn't too hard to do. After all, he spent his days killing people.

Claudia hadn't realized, in all her wandering thoughts, that the doctor was now watching her with barely so much of a

41

blink. Her blood ran cold immediately as she shrunk down into the couch like a mouse. She watched him unfold his legs from his sitting position and take a step toward her, causing the old wood beneath him to creak. The now familiar rush of fear washed over her.

This was it. She was going to die at this madman's hands. It only took so long for him to get bored with her, and this was it. Unable to keep watching her own death walk toward her, she squeezed her eyes shut. Her breath came in hitches, her body shook, and all her thoughts left her mind. Every creak told her how close he was until finally she guessed he was standing right in front of her.

She felt cold air envelope her, as a tuft of her hair lifted from her face.

"Dunce-girl," she began to shake, but refused to open her eyes, "why do they always scream, but you never do?" Her brain was running laps, fight-or-flight syndrome taking over her body. Could she fight? She had felt his strength before. She'd watched him break a ribcage open with his bare hands earlier that day; the sickening crack haunted her mind. No. Fighting back would only bring a faster and more painful death. She would sit and wait, and maybe through her death he would finally find an answer he was looking for. Maybe she'd stop more people from facing unneeded death by an insane man who was searching for answers that were impossible to find.

She felt her hair that he'd grabbed fall onto her face. Then his hands were on her face, squeezing it. She forced her eyes open to find the doctor before her, his right hand squeezing her head as if he'd squeeze out a toy if he tried hard enough. His eyes were cold, manic. She could feel them stab into her soul, dirtying her innocence, destroying what dreams she had. He was killing her with just a stare; he didn't need knives.

The heaviness of her body suddenly sagged against her as it began to shut down. She'd worked herself up far too much for what little energy she'd conserved. She felt her head rest in his hands, darkness scratching at her sight.

No... NO! I'm sure to die if this happens, she heard herself beg her body. It was as if someone else was in charge of it, forcing her to do things she didn't want to do. She continued to watch those eyes as she fell forward, body too tired to listen to its master.

His eyes were still sinking into hers, searching for answers only he could find on his own.

The darkness pained her. She felt so much pain in her frail body that all she wanted to do was give it all up and make it go away. The moment was fleeting, and before she knew it, she was falling head first toward the doctor.

The last thing Claudia could recall was the curious smell of peppermint.

Chapter Five

When Claudia woke, she was still on the run-down couch before the fire. Schnuggles was lying as close to the couch on the floor as it could get, its enormous head awkwardly propped up on it. Without thinking, she reached over and rubbed its neck tenderly. The thought that the thing would awaken made her swiftly withdraw, her heart racing from the immediate panic. But then the thing groaned quietly and rubbed its head against the fabric of the mildewing couch much like a big dog would. Claudia chuckled in spite of herself and reached back over to rub the thing behind its good ear. If it were a dog, perhaps treating it like one would make it like her more.

She continued scratching Schnuggles, matting down the greasy fur and occasionally wiping the stray strands on the dingy couch. After who knows how long, the creature opened its eyes and rolled out its tongue in a pant as its bald tail wagged lazily. She smiled back at it meekly, and gave it a last scratch behind the limp ear before uncurling herself from the couch. She stretched slowly, wondering how long she had to herself until the madman would return to make what was left of her life a living hell.

A sudden thunk from the back of the cabin made the hair on the back of her neck stand on end. Already, her muscles were creaking in pain at the idea of tensing up for another 24 hours, but she had to be ready for anything. Slowly, Claudia stood and looked toward the back of the cabin. If she'd had the strength and courage, she'd try to find one of the many scalpels that were lying about, but they were nowhere to be seen. Even if she was to get one, what would she do? Threaten a man who was more than willing to use them on her? The only "weapon" she had was the off chance that the creature might go berserk, and that thing wasn't about to turn on its master.

Soon after the thunk, the sound of piercing cursing erupted from the shadows. With a tilt of the head, Claudia wondered what he'd done this time to cause himself an injury. To her dismay, it was never anything serious. The first time it had happened, it was nothing but a splinter in his finger. It had taken her two hours to get the damn thing out with all of his twitching and tomfoolery. She knew the doctor hated human contact, but to resist even when demanding someone take out a small thing such as a splinter was just a waste of time- and she had nothing to do with her time, which said something.

Out came the doctor, hopping on his right foot while holding the left in his hand. Occasionally she'd hear an "oh-oh-oh-oh!" mumbled from him as he would almost lose his balance, but beyond that, she only heard intangible mutterings and the pitter-patter of his somehow light-footed bouncing.

He had made it to the kitchen table and was leaning on it when he finally realized she was not only awake, but standing and staring at him intently.

"Ah, Dunce-girl." He tried to stand on both feet in a dignified fashion, but immediately winced in pain and lifted his foot back into his hand. "You awake, yes?"

She bit her lip as she wondered whether or not she should answer. It was one of her least favorite things when he acted friendly to her, and also when he called her that *name*. It was as though they were friends and he'd given her a pet-name. But they were not friends, and he'd be giving her nothing of the sort.

"Yes," she finally murmured as she glanced down at Schnuggles, who was now stretching out like a cat and making its way to stand by her side. Her hand fell to its head, and she gave a little scratch at its good ear causing it to make a sound of content.

"Ah good. Schnuggles was worried," Dr. Cornelious quipped as he put his foot on a chair, now bootless and sockless, to inspect for wounds. It looked perfectly fine to Claudia, and she found herself frowning at the realization. If he couldn't run, and Schnuggles was elsewhere, she could have made a run for it. *To where?!* her mind reminded her, *you have no idea where you are nor how far away town is!*

"So what happened?" she tried drowning out her thoughts

by making any form of sound, and at that moment, that sound was speaking to the madman. Dr. Cornelious looked up at her quickly with an enormous grin on his face, as if about to tell her a hilarious story.

"Well," he began as his hands massaged his poor foot, "was trying to reach a high up spot, Dunce-girl. High, high, HIGH up-" he emphasized with one hand outstretched over his head as far as he could, "-when I finally got it, it jumped out of my hands! Like it had legs. Tricky things, heavy boxes are. Anyway, it landed on my foot with a thud... and, well. Here I am!" Claudia felt her frown deepen.

"I'm surprised you're able to ask... Last night you couldn't even speak." Her breathing hitched as she realized what he had pointed out. Dear God, why *was* she speaking to him? She could already feel her palms become clammy as her knees weakened, threatening to give out. Schnuggles was leaning against her now, pinning her against the couch, forcing her to stay upright. Her mind fiddled with responses, but her tongue had swollen into an anxious lump of nerves. Finally, she regained enough composure to sit herself down again, to hold her now swimming head.

The doctor gave a short chuckle of victory as he finished rubbing his foot, and stamped it down on the floor.

"I had figured as much," he squawked at her before disappearing back into the darkness of the cabin.

~~~

He wasn't particularly built.

On the contrary, he looked sick. One could see rivers of veins that showed through pale, almost luminous skin. The lines in his face were dirty, making them look all the more dramatic. His limbs didn't fit the rest of his body; the arms were too long for his torso, his feet too large for his legs. He was...

Gangly.

Like a rag doll. But she'd felt his strength before. She felt those fingers wrap around her wrist and drag her across the cabin. After watching him, seeing how his body moved, his muscles twitch and lips quirk, she knew he wasn't a rag doll. He was, to put it bluntly, a force to be reckoned with. There was strength in those gangly arms, malice in those skinny fingers.

Sometimes, when she dared to stare at him longer than usual, she'd look for stitch marks. Her mind ventured that maybe Schnuggles was the first Frankenstein experiment, and he was the second. Maybe there was a higher-up madman who fancied himself a scientist.

But even on this night, with his lab coat thrown on the floor and white button-up folded up to his elbows at the sleeve (the shirt, mind you, splattered in what looked like dried blood) she saw no signs of a Frankenstein creature.

Silly, she thought to herself. *There's no such thing as Frankenstein's monster.* But despite her inner reassurance that such things were impossible, she felt Schnuggles, her dog-monster, lick her hand. A shiver ran up her spine as she failed to justify her desperate denial.

Just a few birth defects and gross body parts sewn on by a madman, her voice rang in her head, *and was taught to walk on two feet.* Without meaning to, she sighed agitatedly. This world, the world of this cabin in the middle of nowhere, made little to no sense. She knew what was real, and what wasn't. Everything could be explained with reason... So how, exactly, had she found herself in this situation?

The skin on the doctor's forearm twitched as he glanced up from a notebook he'd been scribbling in, removing a cracked pair of reading glasses from the bridge of his nose.

"Something wrong, Dunce-girl?" he squeaked at her, already fiddling with the lenses with his spindly fingers.

Stupidly, she looked for stitch marks on his fingers again. She chewed her bottom lip as her gaze slowly traced back up to his piercing eyes.

Ah. Those eyes.

The thing that brought the youth back to Dr. Cornelious. His piercing, icy, cold blue eyes. If it weren't for them, she'd have guessed he was much, much older. But something inside them promised youth - a lost youth, but youth nonetheless.

She could taste something metallic when she realized she'd once again bit her lip too hard. She winced as she instinctively brought a hand to her mouth. A mismatched eyebrow raised on the doctor's thin face. A smirk played at the corner of his lip. With one swift movement - he was upon her again.

Her personal space - he loved invading it. He never touched her, yet he reveled in making the girl uncomfortable. He hovered over her once more as he had before, her on the couch, he standing above. He brought his face close to hers until she could once more relish in the only sweet smell in this hellhole - peppermint.

Those weak looking hands, the ones that somehow held so much strength, reached out to her now and took her hand away from her mouth. She wanted to protest, but she found her voice had lost its way. Icy eyes scanned her lips, both eyebrows now furrowed in what seemed like concentration. His lips moved as though he was mumbling to himself, but no sound came out. Claudia found she was holding her breath as her taken hand finally gave up on trying to resist.

Finally, his free hand rose to her face. Gingerly, almost lovingly, he softly brushed her lips. The salt from his skin burned them lightly, but surprisingly, she welcomed the feeling. The minor pain reminded her that somehow, she was still alive. It was a strange comfort to her, and it shot shudders down her spine. Rather than continuing to hold her breath, it had caught in her throat. The sound of her increased heart rate pounded in her ears as she sat, dumbly, waiting for his next move.

His eyes had an almost glossy look to them as he leaned further, bringing the thumb that had caressed her lips to his eyes. Smeared blood sat upon it, and on seeing it, his lips formed a long, deep frown that caused the lines in his face to deepen. The dark shadows from the fireplace flickered on these age-lines, adding years to his otherwise timeless face. It was alien to her, and she felt a twinge in her chest upon seeing it.

They sat like that, Claudia barely breathing and he staring at his thumb, for too long a time. Claudia began attempting to count the seconds as they passed, but her anxiety to his closeness led her to lose count every time she got to twenty-three. Finally, her breathing started coming out ragged. She wasn't giving herself enough air, and she was scared.

Finally, he spoke.

"Cath-" His voice was a whisper that made Claudia gasp in response. She wasn't anticipating that he would speak, so any reaction would have startled her. But instead of continuing what he was saying, the doctor seemed to come back to reality as his eyes darted back to her own. His furrowed eyebrows had risen in surprise, and his eyes had slightly widened. Shock? Why was he shocked?

Glancing at the hand that held her wrist, he removed it as though contact with her skin burned him. His deep frown remained as he straightened his back, the shadows of the fireplace making him look decrepit. The malice was back.

"Don't wind yourself up for no reason," he suddenly quipped. Before she could react further, he moved from the couch back to his chair and sat with an irritated plop; the once swift movements of his body had turned jagged with a silent sneer on his face.

She tried to still her heart rate and calm her rapid breathing as she rested her once captured hand over her chest. The beats of her heart raced like a jackrabbit against her hand. She watched her chest rise and fall with quick breaths and already felt the high of adrenaline wafting through her body to leave her more exhausted than she'd felt in days.

Claudia let herself sink further into the couch; her body felt like it was filled with lead. She didn't know if she should speak or if she should let it be. A quick glance over at the doctor showed that he was already nose-deep in a notebook, his pencil scratching so hard against the paper that the sound bounced off the tiny walls of the cabin. He didn't bother a glance back. In fact, he looked as though he was avoiding looking at her.

So he's a man, after all, Claudia thought to herself, her face growing hot with embarrassment as her mind slowly made sense of what had just happened. He'd touched her. Not just touched her, but he touched her more tenderly than even Matt had.

Ah, Matt. Claudia hadn't thought of Matt for some time now, his soft smile and gorgeous eyes. But then again, as her mind lingered, she found herself thinking of light blue eyes, accompanied by the tingle of her burning lips, rather than Matt's warm hazel ones. If Claudia weren't hot-iron red before, she was now. How was it that somehow, the doctor was even invading her thoughts?! Never mind that he was holding we captive and now made some *move* on her, but she was reciprocating it?!

No no no, she thought as she patted her cheeks with both hands as a means to snap herself out of it. *I am simply lonely and his... Whatever that was... Caught me off guard. I'd prefer Matt over a monster like him any day.* She nodded to herself, still patting her cheeks at an attempt to keep herself in check. The urge to steal a peek over at her captor reared its head, only causing the heat in her face to grow.

I'm lonely. That's all. Silly, stupid me. Stupid Dunce-girl. He's right on that part. With a sigh, Claudia moved her body, turning her back to the doctor. She wouldn't let impure thoughts confuse her only because she sought companionship, which she especially would not solicit from that loon. Curling her legs up to her chin, she leaned herself into the couch and tried to concentrate on Matt. But the more she thought, the more she realized how hard it was becoming to picture her serene life from before. She sighed heavily once more at this realization and closed her eyes. Before she knew anything else, she was asleep.

~~~

Her mind numbed to time. It was irrelevant to her. Occasionally she would wonder how many days had gone by, but only the gradual dirtying of her clothes offered her a sense of time's passing. Her hair was matted and disgusting, for she didn't know if the doctor had a shower in that place. Even if he did, would he allow her to shower? Wouldn't that time alone be too dangerous for her to make an escape? She still had no clue why he had decided to keep her there, but her well-being was an evident priority to him, except for her cleanliness.

Eventually, her hair smelled of nothing but the stink of death. It made her gag every time it would fall in her face. To think some time ago she would have hummed happily at the idea of someone like Matt running his fingers through her hair or brushing it out of her face. Now it was a disgusting thing attached to her head, yet another reminder of the hellhole she was in.

Occasionally, she would awaken from sleep because too much of it had fallen in her face and filled her nostrils. The smell of the knotted clumps of hair was nauseating.

One day, as she was feeling particularly unable to cope with her hair reminding her of the death that enveloped her in this building, she began to cry. At first, it was a quiet sob, her tears falling onto the bald patches of Schnuggles as she leaned into the animal for comfort. If she got a whiff of her hair, she would choke a bit, causing her sobs to become just a bit louder.

Oh, what a bad moment for her to have started doing that. She hadn't known it at the time, but it had been a particularly nasty day for the doctor, and his mood was livid. Today's specimen had proved a little more than he could handle, and he had to kill it on the spot rather than capturing what was going on in its mind. The specimen had spat in his face, threatened him, made horrible insults to his mother (and what a crude thing to assume about one's mother, the doctor had thought), and nearly took the doctor out with a good swing to the face. It had been a horrible experience for him, and he was just cleaning all the blood off his face as he exited the dark back of the cabin when he heard the small sobs of Claudia Boswell.

He approached slowly, like a snake waiting to strike its prey, until finally he was upon her, his hand wrapped nicely around her throat. Claudia tried to gasp but found she couldn't with the air closed off to her lungs. Her immediate reaction was to struggle, but she realized such an effort would prove utterly useless. Why fight against it? She was his prisoner, and if he set her free in death, she would welcome it with open arms.

Her body went limp; her eyes stayed open, and she just stared at her assailant: the madman. Piercing blue eyes shone through a face smeared with blood, those eerie orbs penetrating her with something fierce and dangerous. His face crinkled from furrowing his eyebrows, and yet a manic smile donned his thin, chapped lips. One of his teeth was chipped. She found herself wondering if it had always been that way.

Her throat was so sore. The squeezing of the madman just heightened the pain. But the pain would be over soon, wouldn't it? She would finally find calm in the sweet embrace of death. She wondered when she was last able to relax. Was it that afternoon with Matt? Possibly. Or perhaps it was the morning she had spent with Hannah and Becca. Either way, she looked forward to relaxation again, even if it was in death. All she had to do was close her eyes and let go - let death take her. But her eyes wouldn't close.

Why wouldn't they close?

"Stop," the doctor gasped at her. If she'd had the strength, she would have asked, "stop what?" But instead, she felt her head roll to the side as her vision grew blurry. "Stop now," he repeated, his eyes growing wider. His teeth began to clench as his grip tightened. Claudia felt suddenly weightless as she was lifted from the couch, but the feeling was short-lived as she felt a great force push her away from the doctor.

He'd thrown her into the crackling fireplace. The burning sensation was beyond what pain had been in her throat. By instinct only, she threw herself out of the fire pit, rolling on the ground to smother the flames. Claudia's back sizzled, her skin already peeling from the burn. Had she lain in the fire longer than she thought? It had felt as though she'd reacted immediately. However, the burns… the burns felt so much worse than that. It felt like she'd been sitting in molten lava for hours.

Her tears found her again as she began to sob harder, unable to control herself. Her body shook as she folded herself into the fetal position, screams finding their way out of her chapped lips. The screams were shrill and foreign to her; she had never made a sound like it before. Despite that, finally being able to scream in agony felt good, and yet dreadfully horrible all at the same time.

"Stop crying! Stop making those sounds!" The doctor had truly lost it as he kicked at Claudia. She felt contact on her charred back, causing her to cry out all the more in pain and sorrow. "Stop it, I said!" He was shrieking now, screaming louder than even her sobs. He reached down and grabbed her nasty, grubby, smelly, disgusting hair. The hair that had started it all.

He hoisted her up until she was face-to-face with him again, but this time, he greeted her with a scalpel. She could have laughed at him, she really could have. Threatening her life? She'd just given herself to him, and he wouldn't have it. Instead, he just put her through so much more pain.

Before she could think much more, he was slicing at her hair. Her once beautiful hair was now being chopped away… and she felt relieved.

Her sobs became cries, and cries to hiccups, until finally much of her once beautiful hair was on the ground, save some that hung just above her chin. It was now short enough to not get so dreadfully and nastily in her way with reminders of filth and death.

The doctor was staring hard, his eyes wide. One hand was still holding a fistful of hair to keep her at eye level with him.

That was when she felt it. A twinge of a sort, a smile… perhaps? She felt crazy having felt it. But she couldn't quite describe it in her predicament. She'd have to ponder it on the many nights she'd be left on the couch by herself.

"Thank you..." was all she could muster from this strange feeling that had crept its way into her chest. The doctor stared at her, perplexed. His icy eyes were wide with confusion and possibly a bit of disgust. She just stood, limp to his hold, silent tears still rolling down her cheeks.

"THAT be why you were crying?!" he demanded from her. She blinked back another sob.

"Before you burned me, yes." His only response was to throw her onto the couch by the hair and storm back into his lab to clean the remains of the body in there. She laid where he'd thrown her, unwilling to roll onto her marred back. Silent tears continued their course, as she rubbed the top of her head gingerly, occasionally brushing the hair with her fingers only to sooth herself.

Why couldn't he just kill her and be done with it? How long would it be until she would break into nothing... Why was he doing this to her? For his strange need for companionship? Would he keep her around to leer at her quietly and rub her lips when they bled, just to in turn burn away the rest of her body? Was he trying to train her to be his next companion, much like Schnuggles?

Schnuggles. When she had first arrived, the doctor had spoken to the thing, saying it was the reason she lived. It couldn't possibly be because of the dog-beast... Could it? A quick glance to the wretched thing made Claudia feel sick. Wouldn't it be better for it to die along with her to enjoy the bliss of being away from the monster that was Dr. Cornelious? Despite its terrifying features, the poor thing wasn't evil as he was. It was just an animal (or she guessed an animal) listening to the orders of its master, the equivalent to a pit bull who was trained to be vicious by a dogfighting trainer. It wasn't at fault, and it deserved peace.

She felt the need to snap its neck right that very night. She could feel it already, the crack of the bones telling her that she was finally free, and could run from the disgusting man who seemed only to keep her to torture her. She could easily just walk over to it, pet its sickeningly greasy fur, and with a single pull of her wrists, it would all be over. Instant death would come to the poor thing, and she'd sneak right on out of the cabin, never to see the horrid owner ever again.

The thoughts had only just sprung in her mind when she realized she wasn't planning a double death to set the two free, but a sacrifice for her own needs. Claudia's stomach felt like it was turning inside out as her breaking body threatened to lurch, but she tightened her throat and held a hand to her mouth. She had never imagined herself capable of wishing death on something to spare her life. As she felt the bile creep up her throat, she felt an immense amount of disgust in herself. Swallowing hard, she patted the creature on the head lightly, as it had seemed to notice her displeasure and padded over to lay its head in her lap.

"I've been around that madman too long..." she murmured to Schnuggles quietly. Her voice cracked; it barely sounded like her. "It's like I'm starting to think like him." She swallowed hard again, this time hurting her throat immensely. She'd forgotten she was being choked not long before. She wondered if it had left a mark. With the ache she was feeling, she assumed there was. Not that it mattered; the only two who saw her were the creature and the madman.

With a long sigh to regain her composure, Claudia continued to brush her destroyed hair with her fingers, occasionally wincing at the pain in her back and neck. Silent tears streamed down her face, especially when she would occasionally feel the fabric of her shirt peel away from the burned skin.

Claudia continued to silently berate herself. She knew that if she planned on escaping with her mind, she had to be stronger. But the thought of killing a living, breathing thing, so that she could run away? A profound change was shifting inside of her. It was slowly emerging in the back of her mind as time went on... But she had yet to acknowledge it until that moment. Before the cabin, before the abduction, before all of this, she would have never dreamed of hurting an animal, disgusting or not. She would never have put herself before another living creature. And yet there she was.

Call it survival, Darwin's theory, brain-wash, becoming tainted, or even slowly driven insane by madness itself, but whatever it was, Claudia was becoming *like him*, whether she liked it or not.

And then a more chilling thought sprang to her mind: perhaps a little bit of her always *was* like him.

~ ~ ~

54

One thing Claudia couldn't help but wonder was when on earth the doctor found time to sleep. Did he even have a bed? All she'd seen of the cabin was the decaying kitchen/living quarters combination, and the dreaded examination room. Surely he must have some sleeping arrangement in his own home?

If he didn't sleep, she assumed he must be an inhuman drone who only worked off the sheer madness his brain exuded.

But that's impossible. No one could live without sleep. Her exhausted body was proof of such. But then, when? And how long?

When any other thought was lost on the girl, she would ponder the little things such as this. She wondered if his bed was soft or sturdy, feather or casual pillows? A feather down comforter, or plain sheets? She would daydream of a plush, large bed, a feather pillow ready to take her weary head, warm snuggly blankets tickling her skin and igniting a comfortable glow from deep inside her. She daydreamed about being able to relax, being enveloped in the warmth that only a good blanket could give her.

How she yearned for that kind of warmth. As time ticked away, her skin could only take extremes: icy cold from lack of care, or scalding from a new burn the doctor inflicted on her during his fits. She craved the comfortable warmth of the fuzz on a fleece blanket, the nipping chill of a single foot caught outside of it, then diving back under and relishing in how the warmth would slowly seep through her skin. First only the outer layer of skin would warm up, still cold to her pampered touch, and slowly it would crawl its way inside, filling her with the comfort only cats seem to feel when laying in front of the sunlight.

Fingers tangled in the matted fur of the dog-beast, Claudia found herself once more pondering over the joys of a bed. The doctor had invaded her space far too much tonight, and she was steeling herself away with pretty wishes and thoughts, distracting herself from the sore muscles in her neck. She was sitting much too straight on the mildew-scented couch, Schnuggles's front side draped over her lap, its large hand-paws curled under her legs and its head resting comfortably against her torso. It sighed contently as she found a sensitive spot behind its mangled ear to scratch.

Bed. Comfort. The warmth of a blanket. Claudia could scream in frustration over how much she yearned for such simple things. There she was, daydreaming about it all, trying to remember the details of her own bed likely untouched back in her home.

She pondered if she'd ever be able to sleep in bed again, or if she'd die on the uncomfortable couch that was her new home. With a disgruntled grunt, she repositioned her legs under her body, trying to keep warm under the creature wrapped around her.

And then she heard it.

A little sigh, the smack of the lips. She glanced toward the doctor's armchair, and before her she saw a vulnerable man, sleeping awkwardly with his head rolling from side to side on his shoulders. His shoulders were a bit too hunched over, making him look like he had a hump, but in reality, it was from many days without rest. Whatever the doctor had done before evolving into a deranged lunatic, it wasn't pretty. It had made a broken man with a broken body, fitting to only him and his dynamic.

Claudia waited a few moments, almost in disbelief that the doctor would fall asleep not even five feet away from her. But sure enough, his chest rose and fell with a slow and steady pace, his eyes fluttered and rolled in an REM cycle... He had truly made himself completely and utterly vulnerable to her.

Immediately, Claudia's mind raced. This was her chance if she'd ever have one. To the right of his armchair, there sat a small coffee table filled with scalpels and other surgery equipment, but only the scalpel shone brightly to the girl's eye. All she had to do was get up, walk over, and slice his throat that he had so graciously presented before her. He would bleed out before getting the chance to come after her, making her escape a quick and easy one.

It wasn't like killing something as innocent as Schnuggles. He deserves it, her mind defended. It's the same as when a police officer kills a bad guy. That's right... She'd be justified. A hero even. She would be saving hundreds of people from falling at his hands. She wouldn't be a murderer...

But what about the creature? What would it do?

Glancing down at Schnuggles, Claudia's heart froze. It looked back up at her with green doe-like eyes, likened with the expression of complete betrayal. The girl almost had to catch her breath as Schnuggles stared up at her sadly, its eyebrows raised and a quiet whimper leaving its maw. Her mouth dry, she opened it to give an explanation but cut herself short.

This was silly. A creature such as Schnuggles couldn't possibly know what was going on in her head. However, as though Schnuggles knew exactly what the girl was thinking, it lifted its

56

head and rested it against her chest, right over her heart, giving a loud and heart-shattering whimper of a hurt dog. Its eyes continued to bore into hers, silently pleading that Claudia not do the only thing that would save her.

She wanted to cry; she wanted to scream out in anger. And yet she couldn't bring herself to do either. Biting her lip, she patted the creature's head and let out an exasperated sigh, causing the creature to wag its tail slightly.

They were all prisoners in that cabin, weren't they? Prisoners to their demons. Claudia was the obvious one. However, she had never bothered to think of the creature that had so graciously saved her life. It was a pathetic, yet strangely lovable creature... But it was a prisoner, of its own emotion. While dogs are man's best friend, Schnuggles was something beyond even that. As to the nature of that relationship, Claudia didn't quite know. She knew it loved the doctor dearly, yet at the same time, it seemed to love her in its own childish and pet-like way. It didn't want change; it didn't understand the wrong that was happening in the little cabin.

"How silly I'm thinking..." Claudia mumbled to herself as she continued to run her fingers through Schnuggles's fur. "I'm thinking far, far too into this." And perhaps it was true, perhaps she was. As if in response, Schnuggles gave another whimper and lifted one of its giant paws to her shoulder before sniffing her face, yawning, and lying back down on her lap.

The girl could only sigh again. Even if she wanted to try to kill her captor, she wouldn't be able to move the beast off of her lap. Even if she did, she wouldn't be able to attack the doctor without Schnuggles reacting, and she'd rather deal with the doctor attacking her over the 200-pound dog-beast occupying her lap.

Still, the option lay right before her, and somehow she was guilting herself out of it. How pathetically she was thinking! If she truly wanted to go home, she would slit the throat of the madman before her and begin running.

But then there she was again- thinking just like the doctor would. Kill or be killed. Her stomach flip-flopped. Less than a week had passed since her mind was last visited by murderous thoughts, yet here they were again, back with vigor.

To take a life to save her own... Could she really justify it? With another glance at the sleeping man before her, she made up her mind.

That was it. With very little argument from the creature on her lap, Claudia made her way to her feet and straightened out her clothes. Her palms itched in anticipation as she tried to inch her way to the scalpel that was shining so brightly now in the firelight. Her feet were as silent as a mouse's, and in spite of herself, she was grinning. Before she knew if she'd moved very far, she had the scalpel safely in her fist and was standing before the sleeping doctor.

His chest rose and fell quietly with even breaths, his mouth slightly open. His hands were together, wrapped around his chest in a comfortable fashion, his lab coat still draping around his tiny shoulders. Claudia's grip tightened around her weapon of choice. This was it.

With shaking hands, she held the scalpel with trepidation before the man as though threatening him. Although his breath was even and comforting, hers came in jagged bursts. Sweat formed on her forehead as she attempted to calm her nerves, yet with the tiny surgeon's knife in her hand, her conflicted mind asked herself if she could do it.

To take someone's life. And this time another person's life, not an animal's. Granted, she'd thought of wringing the doctor's neck many times. However, she didn't know if she could do it.

This was fight or flight. What was she going to do?

She watched the doctor's features, shaking in her skin. The girl was more of a lost child than a woman. How she wished someone would swoop down and save her. How she wished to be home, in a warm bed. But that wouldn't happen, would it? The only way she could do it is by taking the life of...

His eyelashes fluttered, making Claudia jump back and clutch the scalpel pointing at his throat. She attempted to make a threatening face, but she knew if he opened his eyes he'd see a scared and desperate little girl.

Although she thought he'd stirred, the man continued to doze, making her sigh in relief. She approached closer, scanning his face for any sign of a possible sneak attack. However, his serene expression showed that he was utterly knocked out in sleep. It was then that the girl noticed how long the doctor's lashes were, as they were probably longer than hers. It gave the doctor a more feminine appeal about him, if he had appeal in his body at all. They curled upward only very slightly and were very, very dark. She had always been so distracted by the piercing blue of his eyes, that she had never really been able to examine the rest of his face.

He had high cheekbones, so high they almost made his face look hollow. She wondered if it was from the very strict diet of nearly no food they were both on. It gave him quite the frail persona, although she knew better. She knew there was strength in that skinny body that would take any attacker by surprise. How he had managed his strength in his tiny body, she would never know. But she had to admit she admired it.

Her eyes followed up to his eyebrows; one was so gray it looked like the entire thing had lost its color, yet she could see little spittles of black peppering the hair. The other was the exact opposite, black with speckles of gray. It gave his entire face an almost uneven look, but it was nonetheless charming in its own way. His eyebrows were nicely shaped as well; it was obvious that before the doctor's body had ruined itself, he could have been a very attractive man. However now... now there was a shell that only left guesses to what he used to be.

His veins, she realized, were what ruined his face the most, so many of the purple and blue things showing so clearly on his cheeks and forehead. One seemed to fall all the way down his right eye, making a teardrop effect. Why Claudia had never noticed such a feature, she didn't know. Yet there it was, the only tear she'd probably ever see come from the eyes of the madman.

Claudia must have distracted herself for far too long because she found a hand with long, slender fingers wrapping around her outstretched wrist. In a panic, the girl dropped the scalpel, which fell to the ground with a soft thump. Her eyes raced up the vein-tear to find that the deep and terrifying eyes of Doctor Cornelious were now open and staring straight at her.

"What you doing?" His voice wasn't angry, only questioning. She watched his normal peppered eyebrow rise as he spoke. Claudia braced herself, ready for the outburst from the doctor, waiting for him to grab her hair, or cut her, or even throw her back into the fireplace. But he waited, holding onto her wrist with a strength that wasn't painful, yet still overbearing. His eyes bore into her, a curious cat looking over its meal before eating it. Yet she waited, and waited, and waited for the pain, abuse, and blood.

It didn't come.

The doctor cocked his head to the side while still staring at her.

"You want learn how to use scalpel...?"

"What..?" The response came out before she could stop herself. Her eyebrows furrowed in automatic confusion.

Oh, doctor. Poor little doctor Cornelious. Reflected in his eyes there lay a genius, yet he was more of a child than he would like to believe. A horrendous killer, who somehow managed to keep the thought process of a child at times, he couldn't even see that she was attempting to murder him.

Or did he? Maybe he wanted to test her, to see how far she'd go, if she'd lash back. She, of course, didn't, but merely continued staring into his piercing, terrifying eyes. The eyes that could bring more fear into her stomach that Claudia had ever felt, yet at the same time, cause the most uncomfortable of butterflies to flutter. Those eyes made her fight or flight responses turn into fight, flight, or stay and endure. The eyes hypnotized her in a way she never thought possible.

They'd been standing in silence long enough to make it uncomfortable, and Claudia shifted her feet. The doctor's grip hasn't loosened on her, and a fresh layer of sweat was forming between their hands, causing Claudia to feel needles poking at her where they were connected. She tenderly twisted it, and the doctor's grip surprisingly loosened.

"Well?" he asked, his hand swiftly finding its way to the armchair while hers fell like a limp noodle. All of his movements were swift, like he was always in a dance and he was the star.

"What?" she repeated, before remembering what it was he was saying. "Oh.. erm... y-yes." Her eyes met the floor; she couldn't bear his gaze much longer.

"Ah... interesting," he murmured. "Maybe when I'm more awake. Maybe then I'll teach you how to use it."

She nodded dumbly as the doctor looked her up and down, trying to make sense of what was going on in the mind of the specimen before him. Her skin crawled.

"Sit down Dunce-girl."

"Yes," was all she murmured as she quickly took her seat on her couch again, close to the creature who before had seemed so abandoned to her.

"Yes..." she murmured again, her stomach turning at the fact that she'd once again failed. She'd failed to save herself from her hell, and she would never go home.

But more importantly, it twisted because the madman who held her captive had just saved her from herself.

And she couldn't help but think he was beautiful while he did it.

Chapter Six

There were times when the doctor would allow Claudia outside, but the occasion was rare. It would usually follow a particularly horrid day of interaction between the two of them. Sometimes the girl would wonder if the doctor was capable of empathy, but the screams from the back of the cabin dismissed the thought entirely.

The first time she was allowed to go out was after the dreaded hair incident, (which already had been a great deal of time for her, since her eyes were already accustomed to being in the dark). It had started with Schnuggles bounding in circles around the door, causing the entire cabin to shake with his excessive weight. Claudia was once again curled up on the rotting couch, peering at the creature from around the couch's back, hands curled around the top. It licked its lips and barked at her happily before doing a few more circles, once again oblivious to its surroundings.

The stink of death was pungent this day, wafting through the house and sticking to Claudia's sweating skin like glue. She had resorted to digging her nose into the couch while peering at the dog, to muffle the smell. Her hair, a mismatch of lengths and tangles, was bobbing itself into messy curls and knots.

Schnuggles was growing impatient as it padded over to the girl and tilted his head to the side, causing the floppy ear to dangle by a strand. It didn't disturb her much anymore, the floppy ear. Instead she found it a nice accent to the creature. Endearing qualities were hard to find in it either way, so she decided the ear would have to do.

Schnuggles wasn't having any of this silent staring, as it probed its nose to one of her hands the way a dog does when it wants attention. Her limp hand was lead up to the top of its head before Schnuggles began panting happily at her. Without so much as a smile, she patted the creature timidly.

The pat must have sent it into hyperdrive, as the creature then began yipping and barking, bouncing between the door and where she sat on the couch. Back and forth, back and forth the creature ran, trying so hard to get her attention. "Outside... outside time!" it seemed to be saying to her. How she wished that was possible, but she didn't even attempt to get off the couch, much less make a run for the door.

That's when the door in the back opened, and out wafted the strongest stink of the house. Claudia found herself choking as she dug her nose deeper into the couch, her eyes glaring toward the darkness. Out came the doctor, looking disgruntled and covered in dry and wet blood. He was mumbling to himself, a quiet squeak, almost like a cartoon mouse when agitated. He approached the kitchen sink that was a few feet away from where Claudia sat and began to fill it with his clothing; first the gloves, then the goggles, then the lab coat. The white scrubs he had donned were only speckled with red, as the outer coat had taken the most damage.

His eyes fell on Claudia, who reacted by squirming lower into the couch, so only her eyes peeked up from the back. She wondered if there was a long pause of silence then, with the two staring each other down, or a mere second. To her, it felt to last a very long time, but time stood still whenever the doctor was in her presence, so the long pauses of whatever were now becoming normal to her.

"Time for some air!" the doctor suddenly sang, gaily sauntering over to the door. His sudden change of demeanor baffled Claudia, as she continued to peer from the couch. He'd made it all the way to the door to join what looked like a dancing Schnuggles when he looked back at her and frowned.

"Dunce-girl," he snapped, causing her to jump out of her skin.

"Yes?" she croaked at him.

"I said, time for some air! You so much dunce, you no know English!" Her heart tugged at her in mild annoyance at him. Despite her tired demeanor, she still hated the name Dunce-girl.

63

"I get to leave?"

"Leave? Who said leave?" The doctor looked at her incredulously, as if she'd offered to eat his first-born. Schnuggles was still dancing at the doctor's feet, occasionally sitting on hind legs to lick the man on the face.

"Outside means..."

"You been in here way too much! Look at you! You look worse than me..." the doctor sputtered at her, "and that says something." He opened the door and stared at her, waiting. At first, she didn't want to oblige, but the waiting sun beckoned to her, begging to see her flesh again.

Before she knew it, she was on her feet and on the porch of the tiny cabin of horrors. She was still under the shade of the porch and found herself almost frightened to be before the sun. Her body wouldn't will her to step out into its glare, toward Schnuggles, who was already rolling about in the dead corn.

"Don't want to go out?" The doctor's voice made her jump, as she'd lost herself in her body's fear toward the light. She glanced over at him; he was sitting on the railing of the porch, an impish smile on his face. Her blood suddenly boiled as she realized he was teasing her. She forced herself to bite her bottom lip to avoid spatting something at the doctor. She didn't want to risk being forced back inside. After all, he was in a good mood for some reason, and she didn't want to test any of it. She just wanted to enjoy the fact she was near freedom for once.

Claudia made herself comfortable on the top stair to the porch, gazing out at the dead corn of the field, her mind at ease for the first time in a long while. In her new found comfort, she went to play with her long hair, but found few strands still met the length she once donned. She frowned at her hair, lamenting what a shame it was to let her long strands go to such a waste. She's been growing it out for so long, and it had looked so beautiful over her shoulders.

"At least it doesn't smell..." she mumbled to herself as she watched Schnuggles come upon a large pile of dirt, which it proceeded to roll around in until one could barely see the true color of its fur.

"Don't know why you're so scared. Look. The sun is covered!" Claudia glanced back at the doctor to see that he had re-entered the cabin to retrieve an apple to munch on. His lithe body was now standing behind her, eyeing her like meat in a store. She instinctively turned to face the doctor so that she could watch him more easily.

"What do you mean?" she asked with a frown, eyeing him suspiciously. The doctor took a juicy bite out of the apple, the crunch echoing off the walls of the tiny cabin's porch. She waited, listening to the rhythm of him chewing his snack, annoyed with the fact that he was continuing to toy with her.

Before the doctor could answer, though, she heard it.

Thunder.

And it wasn't light, off-in-the-distance thunder, either. It was a sudden downpour, we're-hitting-you-out-of-nowhere-thunder. Looking up to the sky, she then realized he was right. What had been left of the sun's rays were gone, and in its place were dark gray clouds. Her heart sunk to the pits of her stomach. Of course he would bring her out on a day like this, why would the doctor ever show any form of decency toward her?

The thunder boomed again, causing shivers to run up Claudia's spine. Ever since she'd been a little girl, she was never fond of loud noises. She always had to watch fireworks from a large distance, she avoided shooting ranges, and storms with thunder left her sleepless throughout the night.

Before she felt as though the doctor had realized her fear, she rose herself to her feet and took a small step off of the porch to reach her hand out. There were no rain droplets as of yet.

"Do you enjoy the rain?" the doctor squeaked from behind her. She cocked her head to glance at him sideways. Another day of his confusing behavior, another day of attempted friendliness.

"I enjoy rain… just not storms," she admitted before looking back to the sky. "And you?"

"Love storms. Love them love them." He was at her side, hands in his pockets. His stature was so casual they almost looked like two friends standing side by side discussing the weather. She continued to keep her guard up, glancing at him sideways from time to time.

"I especially love lightning. Lightning is so … *fascinating.*" The doctor continued."One minute it's there… BOOP! It's there. THEN GONE! Fascinating, fascinating," he rambled happily, a smile the size of a state plastered on his face. "Schnuggles, however, not so much. Loud noises don't agree with him. I bet

65

he'll be huddled on the couch with you tonight." Another thunder boom, another shiver sheared through Claudia's spine. She bit her lip as she continued to hide her fear of something so trivial. After all, she could easily get over this fear. It did nothing to help her while she fought for her life. Thunder was the last thing she had to worry about.

"Here comes the rain." The doctor was still smiling as he watched the sky, his icy eyes twinkling in delight. Schnuggles had made its way over to him, huddled behind his legs and shaking visibly. To see the large beast show fear was so alien to Claudia that for a moment she couldn't pry her eyes away from it.

"Yes yes! It comes now!" the doctor squealed, which finally made the girl look back up at him.

"How do you know?" Claudia asked, but before he could even answer, the downpour began. Claudia's hand was suddenly covered in cold water. She watched the rain, slightly shocked at how the doctor could just *know* it was about to come. She glanced between the rain and the doctor, trying to decipher if he was just trying to mess with her, or if he was trying to show some form of a human side to himself.

"We may not have showers… but we have rain," the doctor suddenly said, still staring at the sky. Before Claudia could react, he glanced at her with a wink and jumped out into the yard of the cabin.

She was flabbergasted. What in the hell was going on? This madman had so many sides to him she didn't even know how to react to half his shenanigans anymore, but this? What the hell was he doing? Trying to be kind? Trying to watch what her reaction would be?

"Dunce-girl!" His screeching yell snapped her from her questions as she found an already drenched mad scientist standing a few feet away from her, waving a ridiculous wave (despite them being the only people for miles). A large, almost maniacal smile plastered itself on his face. She blinked confusedly at him, an eyebrow rising in question.

"Come HERE Dunce-girl! In the rain!" the doctor squealed. "You smell, I smell. WE SMELL. Let's fix that so we don't have to smell!" He was serious.

Boggled, the captured girl took one foot and put it toward the dead gravel in front of her. Immediately it was covered with

66

falling water. It felt so good to her, so familiar. She recalled a time when she was caught in a downpour during a school outing. Becca, Hannah, and she had decided to dance about in the rain rather than try and look for cover. They all ended up with colds the next day and spent it together with soup and Disney movies while Claudia's mother took care of them. Despite herself, a small smile came to her lips from the memory.

Before she could react, Schnuggles had forced her into the rain by pushing her with its large body. For the first time since she'd come to that place, she laughed. The doctor laughed too, as Schnuggles bounded between the two. Claudia was soaked within moments, the doctor already looking like a deranged wet rat. She glanced over at him, seeing the white fabric of his clothing stick to his sickly tiny body. Through the thin fabric of his scrubs, she could see the lines of what could only be scars. It gave her an accomplished rush in her chest, knowing even he'd been hurt in the past. No guilt followed her inner boasting. Instead, she found herself completely enamored with the lines poking through the thin fabric of his clothing. The desire to know what had caused him severe pain tugged at her most curious desires. There was one so large it snaked from the top of his right nipple, down to his belly button. It was long, thick, and honestly beautiful to her eyes. Thoughts buzzed through her head of a failed experiment, one person who wasn't sedated enough, finally getting the slightest bit of revenge on the mad scientist and hacking into his chest with his scalpel.

She realized the thought tugged at her heart. The nagging desire to destroy whoever had hurt him was short-lived, but it was there. She wanted to trace the scars and promise that nothing of the sort should ever happen to anyone, including him.

She wanted to touch it, to feel the destruction of skin cells on her captor. It would confirm his humanity. If feeling his scarred skin would make him seem more human, Claudia felt that she would be able to rest in her prison more easily.

With a start, Claudia realized that the doctor had snapped his hand down and grabbed her wrist so hard that it hurt. Coming back to reality, the girl realized that she had let not only her mind wander but her reactions as well. Not only had she wanted to touch the scar tissue under the fabric, but her body had also motioned to do so without her even realizing it.

For a moment, her mind boggled. The only sound she could hear was the downpour of rain surrounding her. A wet and very curious doctor stood before her. She waited for the moment of his strike. Would he burn her again? Choke her? Or would he find a new way to slowly dismember her will?

Finally, the doctor took her hand and rose it up to his eyes. Claudia's back chilled in anticipation, her skin dimpling, and her stomach churning. What was he doing? Would this be another incident like the night he touched her lips?

He stood like that for a moment, before turning her hand over and inspecting the other side. He searched every finger, every print. It was as if his new project was memorizing her hand.

Finally, the doctor looked back up at Claudia and said, "well, nothing controlling it besides a stupid brain such as yours." He dropped her hand and continued running in the rain, acting like a four-year-old child. "Oh, silly Dunce-girl… She so stupid she don't know how to control her own body!" he squealed to no one in particular, followed by his glass-breaking cackle. She stood, flabbergasted, wide-eyed at him. His reactions were so random that she would never know to anticipate if he was about to strike her, or if he would poke fun at her as if they were buddies from school.

At that moment, it didn't seem to matter. She decided that rather than consistently keeping her guard up, just this once she'd allow herself to relax… even just a little bit. She felt a weight lift from her chest as she forced a laugh out of her once more, and joined the doctor in running to wherever it was he was running.

And that night, for the first time, both the doctor and the captor had fun in one another's company. Claudia didn't even mind the loud thunder much.

~ ~ ~

When the storm had let up, the unlikely duo burst through the front door, still giggling and dripping large quantities of water onto the cabin's wooden floor.

"I will find towels!" the doctor announced as he marched his way to the kitchen and began scavenging through the cupboards. Claudia just nodded as her laughter subsided, a small smile still playing on her lips. She stood there in the open doorway

68

of the cabin, arms now folding around herself in the sudden cold. She doubted that the rain managed to clean them much, but she did at least feel better having been doused in water. She watched as the doctor went through cupboards with wild abandon, throwing pans and canned food all over the kitchen.

Finally, he jumped up with an "ah-hah!" and pulled out two dust-covered towels. He patted them down with some strong smacks and rushed back to Claudia's side to throw one over her head.

"Knew I had these! Knew I did!" he beamed as he began patting Claudia's hair down with the towel. She opened her mouth to protest but stopped herself.

"Now we gotta clean you up and make sure you don't get sick, Dunce-girl." He was almost singing as he made his way down with the towel to her shoulders. "Can't have that can we? Let us step out so we don't track more in here..." He led her back onto the balcony, still patting her as he went along. She just chuckled in response as he sat her down on the first step and handed over her towel at last. She gave him a nod and took it, patting the rest of her body down as he worked on himself.

The quiet rumbles of far-off thunder called to them as the sky cleared. A full moon shone through the clouds, reflecting off the pools of water left in the dead grass and corn in front of them. The night was... peaceful.

Claudia didn't realize that she had lost herself in her comfort until she realized how quiet the doctor had become. The laughter had subsided and in its place... a sad silence.

She glanced his way to see that he was looking at her, and he didn't bother to look away. They were both very close, sitting side by side on the top stair of his porch. He reached out his hand and tucked a stray, wet strand of hair behind Claudia's ear. She shivered at his touch, and his gaze. For just a moment, they were just two normal adults enjoying one another's company after a storm.

He lifted his head suddenly, casting a shadow over Claudia's face. Against the moon, he was nothing but a silhouette. He had revealed a new side of himself. Before Claudia sat a skinny, withering man, someone who had grown old much too fast. She took in his looks, how his clothes clung to his frail frame, making him look even skinnier than he was. She marveled at how vulnerable he seemed to her, and at that moment he looked like anything but a monster. Seeing him was almost pathetic, tugging at the tired heart strings of Claudia.

Once more, Claudia realized that she felt *drawn* to her captor. No, she wasn't so weak willed as to fall for something so pathetic. Or was she? But still, she felt her heart weep for the man before her. The saddest of any song silently waved through his shadow, gracefully stroking Claudia's cheeks in such a gentle way Claudia wondered if she was falling rapidly into madness. Was the monster known as Dr. Cornelious capable of feeling this much pain and beauty?

His icy eyes bore into her skin, leaving marks of pain and hate that will never be seen by any other human eye. For a moment, Claudia wished she could see the man she had grown used to: the one who would grab her by the throat and throw her around until she couldn't move. If he at least did that, she wouldn't feel so much pity for him and so many other confusing emotions. But the feeling was fleeting, as the doctor turned back to his original position and continued to stare at the moon. After a long pause of silence, Doctor Cornelious patted her cheek lightly with his hand and smiled.

For a moment, Claudia considered shying away, but there was nothing to shy from now. If the doctor wanted to hurt her tonight, he would have done so. He'd had one too many chances.

Delicately, she moved closer to him by scooting across the porch. The sound of her clothes rubbing against the wood echoed through the empty field surrounding them. In the distance, what sounded like a coyote responded to the mild rumbles of far off thunder. The wind blew softly, biting at Claudia's bare arms, dimpling the skin in goosebumps. A shiver crept up her spine as she tried to cover herself with her now damp towel. He glanced at her sideways, his face still pointing toward the moon. Her cracked lips stuck to one another as she opened them to try to say something, but nothing came out. She was rendered silent in her state of chaos and confusion.

"The moon is the only thing you can trust," the doctor finally said, his voice quiet. "When you have nothing in the world, and you're down to your lowest moment... The moon will still be there. It will leave you for a day or so, in order to rejuvenate itself. But it will always be back. It's always there, watching over you." Claudia was surprised to hear such words coming from the madman sitting next to her. He was never so serious, except for when it came to his work, but at that moment, she was witnessing a side of him she'd yet to see. The bittersweet beauty she'd seen only moments before was shining through, mocking her and daring her to look further into the psyche of the man before her.

Claudia swallowed hard as she watched the doctor. He never glanced back down to her; he just continued staring at the moon. She traced the veins in his pale face with her eyes, memorizing every line and creating pieces of art using only them. First, she could almost see a heart, then a star...

She continued to search his face, everything so incredibly cold to the sight. Nothing was ever warm about the doctor: the pale skin, the clear veins, the piercing eyes. Everything was so terribly cold. Desperate. Claudia wondered if the reason the doctor was so cold was because of a past he forever ran from, or the loss of a loved one.

What was the creation of Dr. Cornelious?

"Doctor..." The doctor continued his stare, causing the girl to wonder if he'd even heard her. She rested her head against the wooden support beam to her right, glancing from the madman to the moon. "Doctor Cornelious?"

"Hmm?" His voice nearly made the girl blush. It sounded foreign to her. No squeak, no shrill, but a simple hum out of the bottom of his throat, and Claudia *liked* it. The heat of embarrassment grew on her cheeks as she now stared intently at the glowing orb in the sky without so much as a glance to the doctor.

"So..." Claudia cleared her throat. The octave of her voice had risen. "Why are you here?"

"Eh?" The doctor didn't even seem perturbed by her question. "You know. I must find a way to have the perfect person."

"Perfect person?" Claudia nearly cut the doctor off in her question. "What do you mean?"

"It is my belief, Dunce-girl, that once I manage to remove all hate and love from a human mind, along with maintaining free will, I will create a utopia for human beings." The doctor laid his elbows down on his knees and rested his chin on his hands, eyes never leaving the moon. Claudia, now regaining her composure, looked back down at the madman beside her.

"You've got to be kidding me," she retorted.

"Oh, *au contraire,*" the doctor quipped, "what causes all the pain of humans? Hate and love. The two extremities of our emotional scale are exactly what destroy us. They cause pain, jealousy, war, everything that is disgusting in a human being."

"That's just silly."

"Is it?" Finally, the doctor looked down from the orb in the sky back to Claudia, his eyes wide in wonder, energy suddenly filling his aura. "The most splendid of ideas are actually the most simple." Claudia stayed quiet, examining the doctor's reactions, how a vein in his neck would very clearly pump when so much as a little bit of excitement filled him.

Silence hung between them, silence that was so thick a person could have cut it. They sat, staring at one another, confusion swimming through the girl, and curiosity through the madman. There was no fight for dominance, no sarcastic remarks, just brown eyes searching blue, and vice versa.

Finally, Claudia spoke.

"How old are you?"

"What?" The doctor nearly flinched in reaction toward her, flabbergasted by the sudden interest. Claudia relaxed once more around her captor. She turned her body so that her back rested fully against the support beam, and she faced the doctor. The girl pulled her legs up to her chest and rested her forehead against them. A large rock that symbolized all of her fears, pain, and sorrow, tilted and fell from her body. For this night, she was safe. She could feel it. The content feeling in the air, the cool breeze, even the simple expression on the doctor's face told her that for tonight, she was perfectly fine. And he was trying to show her that. The rain, the laughter, the sudden ease in speaking with one another... She gave a simple sigh of relief, the tiniest of smiles creeping onto her lips.

"Your age. What's your age? I'm 21, for example. Or at least, I was last I checked." She didn't bother lifting her head; she was too comfortable. From in front of her, she could hear the doctor shifting his weight around. For a moment, she wondered if she'd overstepped her boundaries with such a simple question and he'd leave her outside... But that would be stupid of him; she could just leave if he did.

"Hmm..." The doctor hummed to himself, and a little sigh came from his direction. Claudia found herself being comforted

72

by the sounds of his breath. He seemed so human. During her time at the cabin, she had seen him as a monster. But to have another human to converse with, to exist with… She needed this.

"I don't honestly know…" She peeked up from her knees to see a deep frown forming in the face of the doctor. "I haven't paid much attention." The doctor chuckled in spite of himself. "All work and no play make Cornelious a dull boy."

The girl's head tilted in wonder at the man before her. If she thought she'd been there for an eternity, how long had he been there? She watched as he put his hands before him and began counting on them, mumbling quietly to himself.

"Well let's see… The last day of birth I celebrated…" he murmured. With a slow lift to her head, Claudia watched as the doctor moved his body until his back was against the wall of the cabin and he, too, was facing her.

"It was.. my 28th birthday that I last remember. But that was so long ago. So long ago…" His eyebrows furrowed as the scientist thought as hard as he could. "I try to forget these things."

"Why?" Claudia rested her cheek in one hand in an inquisitive stance, curious as to how far the doctor would go in telling her about himself.

She was enjoying this. The more he humanized himself to her, the more she'd be able to live at least in mild comfort in that hellhole. It wasn't as though she'd enjoy living in the cabin, but she could at least give her withering body a reason to relax. If she continued thinking of this man as a monster, her body wouldn't be able to continue much further. Her sleepless nights were driving her insane, and her episodes of blacking out terrified her.

In the back of her mind, Claudia was plotting. If she was kind enough to the doctor and he opened himself up to her, maybe she could escape. She resolved to uncover all of his weak points and use them to her advantage to finally run far, far away. Back home. Or better yet, if she were kind enough to him, he would let her go himself.

An undying determination lit up in her chest as she realized if she continued her act, she'd finally be able to go home.

But was it much of an act? In her mind, she wanted to dismiss this all as part of a plot to get away, yet earlier on she had admitted a sort of *attraction*, hadn't she? Granted, this attraction had slowly been growing for some time. From the random moments he would touch her, she knew deep down that something was stirring within- whether she wanted to admit it or not.

"Doctor." The doctor snapped his gaze back up to her as though brought from a trance. "Why?"

"Ah..." The doctor pursed his lips into an "o" shape as he looked down at the wood below them, a look of inner debate plastered on his face.

"Well," he began, "it was so long ago. So hard to remember. It was my 28th birthday. I only remember because she'd drawn a two and an eight on each cheek."

"She?" The doctor looked up at Claudia as though she had a hideous mushroom growing from her skin. "Who's 'she'? You never mentioned a she."

"What was her name again..." The doctor trailed in his thought process, "Carly? No... Cammy? No no... Camille? Claudia?"

"*I'm* Claudia." Claudia felt a rush of agitation toward the doctor. Was he pulling her leg? And the sudden use of proper grammar baffled her... Why was he so serious this night?

"No, you Dunce-girl." Claudia felt as though she had jinxed herself.

"Either way, c-named-girl had a two and an eight on her cheeks that night. That night... That night. What happened that night?" The doctor continued to reach into the depths of his memories, his facial expressions twisting and contorting... Until it all changed within a split second.

Claudia knew that when the doctor did remember, he wished he hadn't. His entire demeanor sagged, his expression fell into a mixture of anger and sadness, his jaw tightened, and he immediately stood to his feet.

"No more moon tonight," the doctor snapped.

"Why?" She blinked up at him, confused, wondering what he could have remembered so suddenly that would change his emotions. What was so severe that it would send someone who killed people on a weekly basis into a state that made his body somehow both stiffen and sag?

"No. More. Moon," his voice hissed. "Get up; it's time for inside." Claudia wanted to question further, but before she could react the doctor had reached down to grab her hair and drag her toward the door. The girl squealed in pain as he dragged her entire

74

weight by a single fistful of hair, from the porch, into the doorway, and to the couch. He dropped her there, and without a word, he disappeared into the depths of the cabin.

Claudia helped herself up onto the couch, rubbing her head instinctively. What had she done to cause such a turnaround? She didn't know.

But for one thing, for the first time since staying in the cabin, Claudia finally slept peacefully that night.

Chapter Seven

The more she thought about the doctor, the more Claudia felt her mind break. Pops, snaps, and other imaginary things echoed through her skull as images of the madman filled her inner eye when she was alone. She would try to enjoy her time when the doctor had disappeared into the dark reaches of the cabin and stayed quiet, but as time went on, he plagued her. The thought of his face brought her both pain and pleasure; his lingering gaze on her skin both burned and chilled it. Her body was battling itself when in reality, she should have been resting.

It grew worse when he was around her. Instinctively, she would shy away from him; he would raise his hand, and she would shrink down into her moldy couch. At times, all he had to do was walk past her to make her breath catch in the back of her throat, or tears to form in the corners of her eyes. Sometimes her heart would flutter and her face flush. Her reactions were all over the place, making her inner turbulence worse.

At times, they would sit in silence. Claudia enjoyed those times – well, as much as one could enjoy the company of their captor. He would sit in his big red armchair, nose buried in papers, books, and notes, while she remained on her couch, lost in her inner turmoil. The thing, Schnuggles, would lie on the ground before the flickering fireplace, snoozing lightly and occasionally groaning from the back of its throat. She would try to keep herself busy with mediocre things: a loose string on her shirt, the feel of Schnuggles's fur between her toes when she used him as a footrest, or even the dances the fire would perform, licking wildly at her and causing her back to prickle in memory.

She could deal with the silent times. Although her body would sit stiffly against the decaying couch, it was the most relaxed she felt since being kidnapped and considering how little relaxation she got, it was something.

However, a simple peep out of the doctor would cause her pulse to quicken and her palms to sweat in anticipation. A simple utterance of "hmmm…" would send Claudia into anxious agitation.

It was unsettling. It was strange. It was flat out unnatural. His voice was higher than anything she'd ever heard from a human. At first, she thought he was doing it on purpose to tease her; however, the screeching equivalent to fingernails on a chalkboard never stopped coming from his mouth. In the beginning, it caused her skin to crawl every time he uttered a word. Now, though, she found it charming in the strangest of ways. Something in the back of her mind would remind her that nothing was charming about his strange voice, but still she found herself smirking at times when he would ramble on and on.

Once, when she felt particularly alone, she tried speaking to Schnuggles in a mimicked version of the doctor's voice. Despite being a petite girl and having a dainty voice of a female, Claudia couldn't even bring herself to imitate the noise that was Dr. Cornelious's speaking voice. Simply put, he spoke much higher and much squeakier than anyone she had ever heard.

It made her feel like he was unreal, like a character from a book, and she would wake up at any moment from a strange nightmare. Yet every time she managed to sleep, when she awoke, she would still be in the cabin, and still hear his shriek from an unseen room.

In her spare time, she wondered what could have caused it. A failed experiment of some sort? Maybe the doctor was a real scientist back in his day, and something had exploded and gotten into his system, causing him to speak forever like a loon.

No, that was silly. Almost as silly as the voice itself.

She concluded that he was simply insane. Nothing else could explain it.

"No." The girl felt a prickle climb her back as she gulped back a yelp, "NO! Why this so wrong? So very wrong!" From his red armchair, the doctor threw down his papers in a huff that only a five-year-old would get away with. "I don't understand why everything go wrong! EVERYTHING!" She jumped at his last exclamation, then tried to force her body to melt into the fabric of the couch. Unfortunately, she was unsuccessful.

The doctor continued to pout; his lips protruded to look more like a duck's bill and his mismatched eyebrows furrowed deeply. He folded his arms over his chest, now staring deeply into the fire, tantrum dissipated, replaced by the deep thoughts of what could only be a deranged genius.

Claudia remained still, wondering what precisely had him in such a huff. She was about to ask him what the matter was when the doctor slowly looked from the fire up to the girl, his furrowed eyes creating new lines on his face she'd never seen before. What she could only describe as an ageless face suddenly looked older than time, but childish in expression. Smile lines stretched on both sides of his face while furrow lines crossed his forehead. She wondered if there were dimples long forgotten on the map of a face he had; however, the thought was fleeting.

"Dunce-girl," he suddenly piped. Against her will, she jumped, and because of her jump, she saw the doctor smile a wide, toothy smile: one that practiced his smile lines, giving a hint to the menacing thoughts possibly playing through the madman's mind. The sound of the crackling fire filled the room as the two stared one another down, icy blue tearing into brown like a hungry animal into a meal. Claudia swallowed, not wanting to look away from the doctor, yet also no longer wanting to look into the eyes that brought her so much confusion. Her hands were shaking at her sides; her shaky breath came in short bursts.

"Still think I'll kill you, hmm?" he finally said, his smile never leaving his face. "Still think I'll make you an experiment? Come now, Dunce-girl; *clearly* I can't make you an experiment. I wouldn't want my first success to be from an idiot brain like yours!" His voice was teasing, his eyes were burning. Claudia finally tore her gaze from him, her body trembling despite her command.

"Too far?" she heard the man squeak. She bit her chapped lips as she wondered how on earth to respond to someone like him. A simple slip-up could send him into a tirade.

"Oh come now, you're *boring*," he finally spat. "What use are you if you never speak to me? I know! Let's play a game."

Claudia couldn't help but raise her eyebrow and glance back at the doctor, who'd now replaced his sinister yet happy expression with a curious one, like what a child looks like when he's trying to find a hidden egg on Easter.

"Do you know games, Dunce-girl? I know games. I know LOTS of games. Although tag wouldn't be a good idea here, would it? With us having very little room, and all... Oh! I know! We could play truth or dare! You girls like that game, don't you? Gives you excuses to experiment, although it's a different kind of experiment I'm used to." He cackled at his joke, slapping one of his knees. "No, that just won't do. I don't want any crazy shenanigans going on this late at night, the neighbors will complain." Claudia couldn't help it; her head cocked to the side, and she found herself staring at the madman in disbelief.

He really *was* insane.

"Come now, Dunce-girl, that was funny!" he exclaimed, causing a smirk to creep up on her lips. The doctor immediately noticed and piped up. "See? You want to play! Now, what game you want to play?" The doctor motioned at her playfully, the look of honest curiosity crawling across his expression. Within moments, rather than looking incredibly old, now he looked incredibly young. His features were almost boyish as he urged his captive to communicate with him. He scooched his bottom toward the end of his chair, leaning both elbows on his knees so he could get his head closer to her.

"Remember how to speak. Reeeemeeemmmberrr!" he urged. "I know you can do it! You may be a dunce, but you're not brain dead. At least, I hope you're not. That would get too boring too quickly... OH! I know!" The doctor suddenly hopped from his seat, with the energy equal to a puppy. From in front of the fireplace, Schnuggles lifted its head, giving the doctor an annoyed look. It made an exasperated groan that seemed to say "well, there he goes again," before laying its head back on the floor and attempting to get comfortable on the rug.

Claudia froze as he fumbled through the shelves stocked about the living room, grumbling words to himself that she couldn't recognize as English, or for that matter, any known spoken language. He fumbled and mumbled, mumbled and fumbled, until finally a squeaky "AH-HA!" came from his lips as he held up what he'd been looking for in glory.

A pack of playing cards.

"Let's play cards," he stated as he plopped himself on the ground before the girl, a wide grin plastered on his pale face. Dumbfounded, Claudia merely stared at him.

"Well?!" he demanded up at her, causing her to jump.

"Right... well..." she mumbled, disturbed by her inability to form coherent thoughts. Although by instinct she still feared the madman, right now she once again found the slightest flutter of butterflies in her stomach. Her smirk was twitching at her lips as she lowered herself down on the floor in front of him, the beast to her right.

"Ah! See? You speak! Good. Good job." He was getting overly excited now, literally jumping from his rump on the floor. "Now you speak more, yes?"

She stared at him with a smile still on her lips as he shuffled the old deck of cards and handed her seven. "You speak more because we play GO FISH! I don't know many other games." He seemed so human that she couldn't stand it. She wanted to reach out and hold him when he was like this, to keep the human side of him around for as long as possible. She didn't want the monster to come back.

The monster.

She regarded his darker side as a "monster" simply out of necessity. In reality, he wasn't a monster at all. He was human, just like her. He had dreams and feelings; he got bored and excited. He played games and played in the rain. And somehow, in his sick and twisted mind, what he was doing was good. He was trying to bring the world a utopia to ensure that its inhabitants would never feel pain again. However, in his quest for something that he would never find, he was putting the very people he wanted to save through the worst hell imaginable.

But why keep Claudia around for so long? She still did not understand. It clearly wasn't because of how "stupid" she was, although that seemed to be the excuse he enjoyed using.

Perhaps he was lonely. No one, not even a madman, could stay in a rundown cottage in the middle of a dying corn field and call himself happy without the companionship of another human being. Granted, Schnuggles was quite the companion to keep. Although, Schnuggles couldn't carry on a conversation, nor play card games.

Despite the abuse, the screaming, the murders, and the experiments, the doctor just wanted someone to keep him company. Before she could think anymore, she glanced at her deck and said,

"Do you have any three's?"

The doctor smiled. Her heart skipped a beat.

~ ~ ~

Fire. It was all she could feel the next morning. She was on fire. The thought that the cabin had caught aflame immediately threw her mind into panic as she thrust herself from the couch before her eyes could even open. Extreme pain, and more burning, suddenly overcame her. She called out, but couldn't even make out what she was saying as she fought through her foggy mind. Her skin pricked and melted with every movement, but she had to move. If she didn't, she would burn alive. Before she knew what was coming from her mouth, she realized she was calling for the creature that slept at her feet. Schnuggles was nowhere to be found. In a desperate attempt, she raised her head up to take a look around but was baffled by what she saw.

Nothing. She saw nothing at all. No fire, no broken cabin, not even a single out of place thing signifying why her entire body was writhing in pain.

From the back of the cabin entered both Schnuggles and the doctor. Doctor Cornelious was in a speckle-free white lab coat, suggesting that the day hadn't even started yet. Claudia's mind continued to panic, wondering what in the world was happening, why it was happening, and anything else that would make it to her muddled thoughts. The creature was already at her side, nuzzling her neck with its nose. She could barely feel it through the searing burn. She doubled over as the fire that continued to consume her began to eat away at her innards. It was as if her body was finally rejecting itself. After all the fighting, and the little food, it was finally shutting down on her.

A noise one could only describe as a desperate gurgle escaped her lips as Claudia mumbled incoherently. The creature, Schnuggles, made worried grunts and sniffs between nuzzling her and running back to the doctor. He, however, stood and stared. It was as if he had a new specimen to admire from a distance. By his reaction, it seemed he had nothing to lose from her pain.

Tears tumbled down Claudia's dirty face, the pain in her stomach growing steadily. What had he done to her? Did the pain have a natural cause or had he drugged her while she slept? If she were capable, she would curse. But at that moment, all she could do was concentrate on continuing to breathe and fight the fire that was eating away at her skin.

Finally, Schnuggles seemed to become fed up with the situation and blatantly pushed the doctor toward Claudia from behind his legs. The doctor scoffed at him in an annoyed fashion, but rather than walking away and leaving the two, he leaned down to touch Claudia.

His hand was like ice, and Claudia welcomed the touch. The second he touched her forehead, she felt the need to press her burning skin against the soothing cool, but she couldn't bring herself to do so. She continued to wheeze and struggle as the doctor poked, touched, and prodded different parts of her body.

"Where does it hurt?" His screechy voice was quiet, almost as though he was hushing himself for comfort. Claudia found herself searching his face. What was his plan? His features were almost sullen, a deep frown creating lines in his pale skin, the sunken eyes seeming much deeper than usual, and the manic ice of his eyes almost twinkling in the darkness. If the madman were capable of worry, that would be what his facial expression revealed. But clearly, he wouldn't be able to hold a human emotion such as that. All he was capable of was murder and insane desires for a perfect human being by poking at the brain.

She tried to turn away from him in defiance, but he immediately grabbed her body and picked her up with one easy swoop. If her body had the strength, she would have fought against him, but she didn't. She fell limply against his chest and felt the sudden comfort of nothing but coldness. Claudia felt as if steam rose into the air as her burning body made contact with his freezing one. She found herself craning her neck so she could rest her forehead against the side of his neck, enjoying the small comfort of something so cold. In her delirium, she didn't notice how stiff the doctor's body had become, and how incredibly uncomfortable he was now acting. Her mind was too muddled with worry about killing the fire within her skin than to worry about something as trivial as the comfort level of her captor.

The doctor continued to carry Claudia until they were in the back of the cabin where a dirty room with a single bed lay. In one corner sat a pile of white and red linen, dirtied lab coats, and what appeared to be clothing from the past week. Beyond that, the room seemed empty to Claudia. He laid her down on the twin-sized dirty bed and covered her with a single blanket. Still in a haze of confusion, Claudia began to argue against the loss of the cold, causing the doctor to frown further.

The situation was growing more and more uncomfortable for him. To him, the one thing more sickening than a human was a *sick* human. To allow yourself to fall so ill with something showed a sign of weakness, in his eyes. The perfect human, his utopia, would exhibit no such weaknesses. He made a mental note to begin studying the immune system more extensively to avoid situations such as this for his perfect beings.

"Hot. Too hot…" Claudia's voice was but a whimper, but it was enough to snap the madman out of his delirious thoughts. As the situation grew direr, he felt less inclined to preserve her life.

"I'll be back with ice." His voice cracked when he spoke, and he walked out of the room faster than Claudia had ever seen him move in the past.

Her head swam, her sense of time spun, and her stomach rolled in on itself as if it wanted to detach itself from her. And the burn of her skin continued to eat away at her, driving her to the brinks of desperation. Would this burning fire finally bring the release of death? A little voice inside her hoped it so.

The doctor returned in what seemed like years later, but it only could have been a few moments considering the size of the small cabin. In his hand, he held a simple ice pack. It looked like some animal hide, and due to the awkward square-shape coming from within it, Claudia could guess it was full of ice. The top was screwed shut with what looked like a bottle lid.

Before Claudia could ask what was happening, the doctor applied the pack to her forehead and pushed lightly on her shoulder to make her lie down. She hadn't even noticed she had sat up. Did she have any control over her body? His hand against her shoulder was freezing cold, but at this moment, very welcoming. The ice pack felt awkward and spongy against her forehead, but also was enjoyable. Her mind continued to spin, but before she could say anything, she could hear the doctor whisper, "try closing your eyes, it will help." As she closed her eyes, all she could think of was how much different the doctor sounded when he whispered. She'd never heard anything from his mouth except for his high squeak of a nails-against-a-chalkboard voice. For a moment, the husky whisper almost sounded like a normal man's voice… But that must be the fever talking. Fever. That's what she had. She could hear him whispering further, explaining he was trying to break it. Without even trying, Claudia groaned in dismay. How did she have all the horrible luck in the world? Why couldn't she just die quickly, like the rest of his captors, rather than be stuck in a situation like this? Her mind continued to tumble into an abyss of confusion.

With her eyes closed, Claudia began to think of only one thing: coldness. She longed for more cool things to touch her. The first thing she felt was whatever was on her shoulder. What was it again on her shoulder? With the fever fast eating away at her thoughts, she couldn't remember. But before she could think otherwise, her body reacted and nuzzled whatever it was between her cheek and her shoulder, enjoying the small sensation of anything that wasn't burning.

The doctor, however, was not amused by this reaction. His body once more stiffened up, and his frown now became a sneer as he twitched in annoyance. That single point of contact between Claudia and himself made his skin crawl. His hand felt as though an entire infestation of ants had laid a nest under his nails. His first reaction was to beat her so hard she would forget the entire night and suffer from amnesia. But beating someone already in such a pathetic state was even beyond this mad scientist.

He sat awkwardly with her for some time, pondering how on earth he would free his hand from the sickened girl below him. About half an hour later, he realized she'd fallen asleep. It wasn't a peaceful sleep, but it was sleep, nonetheless. Softly, he removed his now burning hand and immediately stepped away from the bed as though his life depended on it. Before he could react further, he slipped out of the room and cleared Claudia from his mind.

She had a dream.

In the dream, she saw a madman who lived in a cottage in a field unknown to any civil city. He lived on his own and seemed to enjoy every minute of it. He had a pet dog, although the dog wasn't very much of a dog anymore, more of a thing. The two lived very happily in their little cabin, and then one day the dog-thing brought Claudia to their happy cabin. That's when she found out the madman in her dreams didn't live quite the happy life. On the contrary, he lived a morbid life. His life was full of death and malice, his activities all murder and experiments, and his heart long dead to emotions of the average human being.

She dreamed that when she was brought to this little cabin, she was tortured. Her back was covered in welts from burns of the fireplace, her hair was hacked off by a scalpel, and her skin was adorned with cuts and bruises from random assaults by the deranged man. She dreamed that she could feel her mind break day by day, losing touch with reality and the hope that she'd be found and instead growing accustomed to the beatings, and fond of the few acts of kindness the madman would show her.

She dreamed this entire dream, but all the while knowing full well she would wake up. The comfort of waking lay quietly in her head, tugging at her heart strings when she most needed it.

And on waking from this dream, she smiled in spite of herself and snuggled deep into her pillow. She found herself chuckling and wondering why she would dream something so sinister. It was perchance all the horror movies she watched. She noted that she'd stop watching them before bed. Especially when sick. Wasn't she sick when she fell asleep? Oh no, that was the last part of her dream. She ended the dream being sick, and the madman had taken care of her.

Oh, that madman. Her fingers twitched as her mind switched back to the thought of the man of her dreams. Everything about him had been so vivid... As if he were all real... He even smelled like... What was it again?

Instinctively, she sniffed. Ah yes, that's right. Peppermint. It was all around her even as she laid in the comfort of her bed. What a queer smell for a murderous person to have lingering on their breath. She wondered if there was some deep meaning behind it that her subconscious had thrown in...

And then she noticed it.

Peppermint. She only remembered peppermint because she could *smell* it. It was everywhere around her. In her hair, her clothes, on her pillow...

Her pillow.

Claudia's eyes finally opened from waking from her fever-induced dream and took in her surroundings. Immediately, the girl wanted to kick, scream, and cry. Nothing had been a dream... Nothing at all.

There she lay in a strange bed and in a room she'd never seen before. When she tried to hoist herself up, she was met with a sense of dizziness so extreme that she wondered if she would vomit.

Once she managed to prop herself up with the peppermint-scented pillows, she glanced around. It was a plain room. The walls were still of the same logs from which the rest of the old-timey cabin had been built. On one end of the room, near the door, there was an antique looking wardrobe. It was quite beautiful, made of a fine, deep, brown wood. The legs were dragon claws, and the handles had so many carvings in them, they looked like angel wings. Claudia wondered why the doctor would have such an ornate thing in his plain cabin. It was so out of place.

To her left lay a simple bedside table. There was a candle inside a holder laying upon it, half burned away. When Claudia touched the candle idly, she noticed the wax was still soft from having been blown out not too long ago. She was going to retract her hand until something just as curious as the wardrobe caught her eye. Under the bedside table, as though it had been stashed there to stop anyone from finding it, was what looked to be the corner of a box. Claudia, not even thinking in her already sick state, reached down from the bed to grab whatever it was hiding below the table.

In her hands laid a dainty, but beautiful, wooden box. It was dirty and light gray, causing Claudia to wonder if it had been white in its prime. Upon lightly rubbing the dust away, Claudia found light purple details across the ridges of the box. The details were swirling into purple vines, and upon them were white lily pads. On the back of the box, there was a crank, leading the girl to believe that she was holding onto a music box. There was a silver latch on the front that looked beaten and torn, as though the user had opened the box so often they'd broken it. It was dainty, fitting on her hand with only the corners peeling off. Although dirty and old, none of the paint had chipped off, creating an old yet completed feel to the thing. Claudia wondered if music would play if she opened it. Would it? She was curious what kind of music would even play out of a box that Dr. Cornelious owned. Better yet, why did the doctor even have this thing?

Slowly and delicately, she undid the latch and gingerly opened the box. Not a peep came out of it. With a small sigh of relief, she opened it the rest of the way to find a deep red velvet lining the insides of the box. It was simple, but simple in a majestic way. Inside the lid there was a dusty, broken mirror; one wouldn't even be able to see their reflection in it with all the abuse it had seen. However, what caught Claudia's eye the most wasn't the broken mirror or the pretty velvet. On the contrary, it was the paper that was tucked between the mirror and the wall of the box. The paper was old and wrinkled. Some of the ends looked burned and ripped, and what was on the paper?

A black and white old fashioned photo. Like one Claudia had seen of her parents and grandparents, only in much worse condition. The picture was of a young woman that was smiling at the camera, yet seemed as though she wanted to do the opposite. She wore a white bodice, and her eyes were big and wide, like a deer. Her hair was fashioned into a big curl in her bangs, the rest waving out from her shoulders. She was beautiful, but something about her seemed to cry out to Claudia. There was a strange tiredness to the woman, as though she'd aged well beyond her years and wanted nothing more than to rest. There were small bags under her eyes, but they were only noticeable if you squinted at the picture.

She looked much like Claudia did.

Despite the twisting of her stomach, Claudia found herself examining this picture very closely, sucking in every detail she possibly could. The woman's smile seemed so practiced, as though she'd done it day in and day out. How long had she been practicing this smile? And for whom? Why? The woman seemed so pained and hurt. Was she the last person that the doctor had imprisoned? Did that mean Claudia wasn't the first? She felt the need to weep for the woman in the photograph but felt she had nothing to offer.

If she were the last woman, it would explain everything. Why the doctor kept her, that is. He had a certain taste for female companionship and continued to satiate that need. Claudia was nothing but a look for him.

Suddenly, the bedroom door cracked open. Claudia slammed the box shut and shoved it back under the bedside table. She didn't have time to adjust it just as the doctor had left it, but she needed to get it back in case he reacted badly toward her knowing about it.

The doctor was standing in the doorway, looking more awkward than she could ever remember him. He stood for a moment, glancing about the room until his eyes found her. She blinked back at him, her body stiffening despite still lying in comfortable blankets and pillows. There was silence between the two, giving Claudia time to calm herself down. But still the questions continued to buzz in her head. Who was that woman? Was she the last woman that stayed in this horrible place? Why did he keep them here? Because of taste? Why did he need to keep people around when all he would do is torture and hurt them?

Torture and hurt. The last question left a bad taste in Claudia's mouth. As naïve and terrified as she was, she couldn't say that all the doctor had done to her was torture and hurt her. Yes, a majority of it was… Yet, here she was in his bed and without a fever when the last time she'd been awake she thought she was dying.

He is a horrible monster! her mind argued. He was only keeping her for whatever sick plan he had. The same plan he had for that girl! She felt disappointment swell in her chest. All the little moments they had shared together... It was all a rouse.

Why would he care for his little pets? The only pet he cared for was Schnuggles. And she was no Schnuggles. Nor was that woman. They were something else.

No, he wasn't caring for her. He was plotting. Plotting for what, she didn't know, but his "care" to make her better had nothing to do with goodness in his heart, for he had none.

"You feel better, yes?" The doctor was still in the doorway, wringing his sleeves in his hands.

"You'll ruin your coat if you do that," Claudia responded, still trying to maintain her composure. Her skin prickled. How exactly would they leave this situation? She felt as though the only way was through the fireplace after the madman had beaten her.

"I make more," he dismissed. "You feel better, yes?" He leaned his head forward on this "yes," looking more like a child asking for a sweet rather than a madman making sure his kidnapped victim wasn't dying from a fever.

"Yes… I feel better," she responded uneasily. "If you want I can go back to the living room."

"Yes. That would be good." The doctor nodded at her.

As Claudia swung her legs from the side of the bed, she realized that whatever she'd done... She'd done something horribly wrong. The awkward stature of the doctor went from innocent and strange to angered and insane within a split second. The ends of his lips twitched, his eyes narrowed, his breath hitched. She froze immediately, hoping that whatever she'd done she'd stopped, and that hopefully she'd avoid a beating if she held perfectly still.

Seconds passed, the next more painful than the last, but the doctor never approached her, he just stood, looking angry and distorted. Claudia wondered if it was her mind applying the look toward the madman, but she decided that if she didn't apply such a façade, she would go mad and treat him like an average human. *Like I stupidly have been*, her inner voice bitterly reminded her.

Slowly, the girl lowered herself to the floor and stood. Still, the doctor didn't move. It was now that Claudia realized he wasn't looking at her face, but rather her feet. Upon glancing down, she realized she'd lightly kicked the little music box she had been admiring not even a few minutes ago. Claudia's mouth went dry. Did she act surprised? Should she pick it up and ask what it was? If she dismissed it what if he caught on that she'd gone snooping in his things?

Her breath grew ragged in panic as she glanced back up at the doctor. He was still in his original spot, staring intently at the little box by her foot. His angry eyes still slit, his mouth pursed, lines formed on his face. She wanted to run, but the only escape was right past him.

"Erm..." was all that came out of the bewildered girl's mouth as she glanced between the box and the doctor, "I'm uh—sorry. Didn't see that there-"

"Did you look?"

"What?" His voice had taken her off guard. It was in a whisper and almost had no pitch whatsoever. She knew his usual high-pitch-squeal was there, but the whisper was so breathy her ears could barely catch it. She instinctively moved away from the box, toward the other end of the bed.

"L-look at what?" she questioned. "At what?" Her mind was screaming in fear. She didn't want to go back into the fireplace. Her back was already burning at the thought of being thrown into it again. The fear of the fire licking up and down her skin, causing bubbles and scars that would never fully heal was something that was fresh in her memory, and seemed never to leave. She cringed instinctively as the doctor took a single step toward her.

"Did... you look in the box." His words were hollow; his eyes were empty.

"That's a box?" she tried desperately. "Sorry. Didn't know."

In a quick motion, the doctor was upon her, pinning her against the wall across from the bed, his hands squeezing her wrists so hard she knew they would bruise. His chest was hard against her own, his breath thick on her face. Her hands had been thrust beside her head to pin her easier, and in the moment, Claudia was bewildered by the sudden touch of the doctor.

His body was so warm. She could feel his racing heartbeat through his chest, his ribs poking through his muscles as if there was no fat on his body. His hip bones were driving against hers, so painfully she wondered if he even realized how close he was pushing against her.

For a split second, there was warmth, everywhere warmth. The delusional state of Claudia's still sick mind begged for more human closeness. For this lost moment of her sanity, she wanted to moan and buck back at the doctor. How long she'd gone without so much as a human hug or any other passion. She wanted it suddenly, nearly craving it. The carnal desires from within her were lashing out, clawing, kneading, begging, desperately trying anything it could to make their way to the surface. Suffocating on her delirium, the victimized girl closed her eyes to attempt to collect herself, but she couldn't. She felt the fingernails of the doctor stab into her skin, the smell of peppermint enveloping her like a closely knit cocoon. She bit down on her chapped lips so hard she felt herself swoon in dizziness. Her body was feeling desperately needy. The heat was now burning her slowly, more than the fireplace did to her back. She found herself gasping for breath, and when she opened her eyes, she wrenched away from the doctor.

She found herself with her belly against the wall now. The doctor took her reaction as a chance to pin both arms behind her back and slam her against the wall so hard that her eyesight grew blurry. She found it hard to breathe. It felt as though the doctor was sucking out her life.

"Did you open it?" The doctor's voice dipped menacingly, the usual squeak buried under what seemed to be the growl of a questioned alpha. "Did you?!" He shook her tiny body, her forehead rattling against the wooden wall. There would be a bruise later, she noted to herself. She could almost feel it forming already.

"I don't know what you're talking about," she muttered in a daze, head still ramming on the wall repeatedly.

The doctor came to an abrupt stop, but he held the girl against the wall still. There was silence; not even crickets were chirping from outside the cabin. Claudia strained her ears, trying to listen to the madman behind her... but all she heard was his breath.

She waited, because waiting was all she could do in this predicament. Fighting against the doctor would just re-anger him, and if she had to wait out his moment of instability to escape a beating, she'd wait the entire day if needed. She felt the doctor's hold on her arms lighten for a moment, then shudder away from her. She stood, still as she could be, waiting for a response. None came.

Claudia lowered her arms to her side with her forehead still against the wall. Her ears still perked, waiting for any form of reaction from the doctor. Her blood pumped hard in her chest; she could only think that the worst was about to come. His hissy fits of random abuse never ended well for her. Her hair and back were proof of that.

Suddenly, there was a force around Claudia's waist. She was pulled back from the wall, and into something warm. A flush heated her cheeks as she was reminded of her carnal desires that hadn't even ended a few seconds past. What was happening? Was he going to rape her? What's worse, would she *enjoy* it? This sort of behavior was so strange for the doctor that Claudia had lived with the one comfort that he'd never rape her. The very thought of touching her would send him into a spiral of cringes and insults. No, rape had never been an issue with this captor. But now, here she was, having been carried by none other than her self-loathing captor to sleep in his very own bed, and now being held against him as if...

As if what?

"Catherine..." she suddenly heard. She felt skinny arms wrap closely around her waist from behind, and hair brush her neck. The weight of a head resting on her left shoulder pushed down on her, making the girl gasp quietly in surprise. Against her back she felt his chest, warm and so very bony: comforting yet uncomfortable.

"Oh, Catherine this is all so very wrong." The doctor's voice was a whisper in her ear; his arms held closer to her body. "You shouldn't have left me, Catherine. What a mess I've become. What a mess."

Again, Claudia felt confusing emotions for the doctor: pity, curiosity, and even buried beneath those, worry and care.

Yes, she realized, she cared for the doctor. She'd come to worry for his well-being. She wanted to know why he ticked the way he did. She yearned to help him defeat his inner demons. She wanted to kiss up his scars and protect him from whatever it was that had hurt him. But most importantly, she wanted to lay with him the way any other man and woman laid together. She wanted to enjoy the arms he had around her and ignore the fact he called her by the wrong name.

But then something sparked in her mind. Hadn't he said something similar in the past? Immediately, the memory of his first tender moment with Claudia came to mind. He'd nearly said it then. But he'd stopped.

Cath. Catherine. He's nearly called her Catherine.

This realization left a bittersweet aftertaste in her mouth, only giving clues to the questions she craved to ask, but also leaving her bewildered as to whether she wanted to know the answers. Her heart strings throbbed, her eyes pricked in threat of tears.

And then Claudia had to ask herself:

Who was Catherine?

Chapter Eight

What a mess he'd become, indeed. Claudia's mind was screaming as she fought with herself, unsure of what her reaction would be in response the doctor's sudden affections. This was the exact opposite of any form of treatment he'd ever given her. Had he finally lost his mind completely?

Her body was stiff; her fists clumped together at her sides. She waited for a reaction from the doctor, for him to realize what he was doing and throw her away from him in disgust. But nothing came. He continued to hold her around the waist, his chest to her back, his heart beating softly against her.

Breaths left her in shudders as she counted his heartbeats, her eyes closing in concentration. Her body was warm, and despite how tense it was, comfortable. She tried reaching into the depths of her memories, wondering when was the last time she'd felt this warm, but she couldn't quite remember. Not this warmth. Not something so raw.

Raw is the only word that explained what she felt right at that moment: pure, sheer, *raw* warmth. Her beaten body, her permanently scarred back, her tattered hair, her tired eyes, her prickling fingers… warmth she would never be able to explain with words was filling her, encasing her, enveloping her, *eating* her. She worried that if she opened her mouth to utter a word, her breath would shake and shatter what was happening. It was too beautiful of a moment to destroy. No, she would sit and count his heartbeats, and enjoy the warmth spreading throughout her body.

Every time the doctor breathed, the breath would brush her skin, causing her flush to deepen. It tickled at her hair, licked at her earlobes, and slid across her neck tantalizingly. Still, the girl didn't move. She was much too lost in both enjoying the warmth of her current situation, and asking herself:

Why was she enjoying this?

This man, the one that was holding her so gingerly at this moment, was a murderer who had been holding her against her will for the past who-knows-how-long. She had watched him kill hundreds of people for the sake of his irrational science, turn people into things that begged for death, and lived in the delusion that he would somehow find a utopia hidden behind all of it. He'd thrown her into fires, beaten her, cut her, and broken every single part of her body either physically or emotionally. He'd taken Claudia Boswell and made her into a worm. A once-average girl, who enjoyed bars, social life, and stories of petty drama, had become a machine who only worried about her survival... And the survival of the doctor.

Standing in his arms was making her realize one thing: The doctor was slowly becoming her world. It wasn't that she embraced his choices in life, or his personality for that matter. But he was all she had. Schnuggles was one thing, but it was a pet, something that would pass in time due to nature. However, for as long as she stayed in this world where time stood still, the doctor was her only companion.

She needed him. In the beginning, she wanted him to disappear, but now, she would crumble without him. The reason she wasn't writhing away from the madman at this very moment was that she needed him just as much as it seemed he needed her.

She softened to his touch now, dropping her head back to rest on his shoulder, closing her eyes as she felt a large tension leave her body. The doctor continued to hold her, mumbling every once in a while. Occasionally Claudia would hear him say "Catherine" again, and she accepted it. It would be all too surreal to hear him say "Claudia." She didn't know if she was important to him as a person, as Claudia, or if just having another person around was important to him. It didn't matter to her at that moment; all she cared about was the fact that the doctor was finally touching her. He was making her feel important.

They stood like that for some time, the doctor mumbling

to himself, his grip occasionally tightening around Claudia's waist or loosening, but never falling, and her trying to memorize every detail about this moment to keep herself going on the harder days. The smell, the feel, the raw warmth... she wanted to keep it all locked up in her brain, so that when she needed it, she would have it.

Finally, the doctor's warm hold disappeared from Claudia's waist, and before she could turn around to say something to him, he was already gone. A twinge of disappointment tugged at her as she bit the bottom of her lip, feeling the cold of the air creep through her clothes to her skin. It would be a very long day now.

She walked quietly toward the door, almost on her tip-toes in anticipation of a sudden attack from the madman. When she reached the door, she braced herself for a hand to grab her hair, or something to hit her upside the face. Nothing came. Instead, she stood at the open doorway and peered about, curious as to where the doctor had so suddenly disappeared.

The girl was about to give up and tip-toe back to her couch in the living room when the doctor's head suddenly appeared from the doorway; his work goggles were already strapped to his head.

"Get some clothes from the closet," he said to her quickly. "Your old clothes are barely even rags." And with that, his head was gone and the door made a loud click, implying that he'd locked it behind him. Not that the girl would go after him right now, he was clearly at his wits end with his emotions, and she wasn't about to try her luck.

However, he was right. Looking down at herself, she realized that her clothes, once a nice pair of blue jeans and a swanky top for bar hopping, had been ripped, burned, stained, and all around destroyed. The jeans were torn and frayed at the bottom, holes in both legs in random spots from cuts and burns of the doctor, and her shirt was barely holding on by a few intact strings in the back from the burnings of the fireplace. She frowned at herself. She looked like hell. Although, in this place, appearance was the least important thing to worry about. She stayed in the doorway for a few moments, waiting to see if the doctor would change his mind. He didn't.

With that, she carefully walked back into the room toward the old wardrobe that she'd noticed earlier. Approaching it, she noticed once more that this was something much too fancy for the doctor to own. It was a dark wood, carved to perfection by its maker. There was a gloss finish to it, making it shine in even the smallest amount of light. The handles were shaped into dragon claws reaching out and holding themselves to the door; the door carved into a scenery one could only find in a child's storybook. Claudia found herself running her hand over the wood before bothering to open it. It was smooth but covered in dust. The thing hadn't been so much as touched in years, it seemed. When she went to open the door slowly, it creaked slowly and loudly. She wondered what she would even find in a wardrobe that the doctor never touched. Needless to say, the girl was surprised.

Inside the wardrobe hung a variety of older, but pretty looking dresses. They reminded her immediately of what her mother and aunts wore when they were her age, complete with poofy shoulders and flower prints. She ran a hand over all the dresses, causing a cascade of dust to fall from them. There were so many of them that Claudia wondered if they were the clothing of victims that the doctor stripped.

Or of that woman.

The waterfall of realization hit the girl just then.

Catherine.

The picture of the woman.

The untouched wardrobe full of pretty dresses.

They must have been the same. These must have been her clothes.

But the question remained: who *was* Catherine?

Checking the door for the doctor, Claudia slipped her way back over to the bedside table to gingerly pick up the music box. She unclipped the latch, swung open the fragile thing and snatched the photo out from its place between the mirror and the lid. She wasn't interested in looking at the tired, wide eyes and the practiced smile of the woman in the picture. Instead, she immediately flipped it around.

"Catherine – 19xx" the picture read, except the last two numbers of the year was so badly worn out she couldn't read it. Claudia's mind began to jumble. Her heart panicked.

Catherine. He had been speaking about a Catherine. What had he said? Claudia could have cursed herself for forgetting what it was that the doctor had been mumbling to himself. She'd been much too worried about memorizing the feel of his arms around her waist and his chest against her back.

She found herself sitting on the bed, her eyebrows furrowing in thought as she stared at the name and date on the back of the photo.

C-named-girl had a two and an eight on her cheeks that night, the same night that the doctor couldn't bring himself to discuss. Catherine. She was what the doctor didn't want to think about.

Claudia felt a pang of jealousy then, wondering what it was that this woman had that she hadn't, and why she had such a practiced smile on her face. Her curiosity turned to resentment as she realized what the doctor had been trying to protect so badly, this picture of this woman. What made this woman so important that he'd keep all of this. More importantly, why did she and Claudia look so much alike?

She placed the picture back in its place, closed the box, and placed it back underneath the bedside table. The wish to destroy the picture burned in her chest. With a deep frown plastered on her face, she glanced back at the opened wardrobe full of pretty little dresses.

These were Catherine's. They had to be *that* woman's dresses. And yet the doctor had them. Claudia's stomach turned itself in her fit of jealousy as she cautiously made her way to the wardrobe.

Did the doctor beat Catherine? Did he leave scars on her back from countless nights in the fireplace? What about cut her hair? It didn't seem that he did that to her; in the picture, she had pretty long hair that was primped and preened for the picture. She felt a bitter taste in the back of her mouth as she approached the wardrobe again, this time taking her hand to glance between the dresses, her nose wrinkling at each one.

Catherine had horrible taste in clothing, Claudia decided. It was as if she shopped with Claudia's mother when she was young. Claudia hated it. She glanced here and there, picked some up and pushed them against her dirty body, and finally ended on a simple enough dress with poofy short sleeves, a cream background, and pink lilies embroidered on the bottom. She knew it would likely grow dirty when she wore it, and half of her hoped it would.

The dress fit Claudia so well it almost startled her. It was tight in the chest area, making the naïve girl beam in pride for a second or two, but realized it did her no good considering the doctor seemed to be the most asexual man she'd ever met.

Either way, was she honestly jealous of some picture of this woman? Yes, the doctor was important to her. At least, she felt he was, given all of the sudden realizations and feelings she'd recently discovered. Yet would she dare suggest that she desired a romantic type of attention from him? A small voice in her mind harrumphed like a child and stated that, yes, she wanted all of his attention. She wanted the doctor all to herself. After all, she'd been here long enough to earn the right of having the doctor all to herself, hadn't she? She'd dealt with the beatings, the burnings. She had lived through the fear, and now she'd even learned to smile. She'd learned to enjoy the warmth that the mad scientist's body gave her when they touched. She'd learned to live in all these ways. She deserved for him to be hers and only hers.

Claudia's mind was breaking.

The poor girl just didn't realize how much.

But she would know soon enough.

~ ~ ~

There was only once that Claudia entered the darkness on her own accord. She had long since deemed that area to be the doctor's "special area." Much how he never sat on the couch, she would never enter the darkness. She felt no need to go back there. After all, that's where all the screaming people would go. There was one incident when Claudia had witnessed the doctor drag a woman into the back, all the while the woman begged Claudia to help her. In the past, the blood in her would have had run cold as she would shield her eyes into the couch.

Now, though, she watched with a sick sense of curiosity, wondering if the doctor would finally manage to do whatever the hell it was he was trying to do (perfect human being my ass, she'd often scoff to herself). Nevertheless, she vowed she'd never enter whatever chaos the dark room was.

Until one day, she was forced to.

She was sitting on the couch, idly flipping through one of the many water-destroyed books that littered the floors of the cabin. It was another medical book that was far beyond anything the girl could understand, but it helped pass the time in the day

98

until she had either Schnuggles or the doctor to interact with.

And then she heard it. At first, all of the sounds were muffled, but the distinctness of the sound made her ears perk. It wasn't until Claudia realized she was hearing the doctor scream that her body moved without so much as a command from her brain. Past the couch, through the kitchen, and into the darkness she ran, heart pounding and adrenaline pumping.

His scream continued, and from what she could hear he was panicking. She couldn't make out the words; there was too much muffle behind it all. She felt around in the darkness, hands feeling for door knobs to rooms she'd only seen a limited number of times.

Then she heard another scream, and a huge "thunk" to follow it. By now, she was full-on panicking, complete with hands shaking and mind screaming.

"Hello? Hello!" she was calling, fumbling and feeling for any door in the dark. Finally, her blind hands found one, and she flung the door open.

The pumping inside her veins was painful from adrenaline as Claudia stared down the man before her. He was much taller than she, and dark skinned. He had an exotic look to him, and a feral look in his eyes. He was a survivor, something far beyond Claudia could have ever been. She always knew she was pathetic in most cases; he just made it obvious that she was.

It was clear what had happened. The room was mostly empty, except for a table, a gurney full of old-timey looking medical items, an unconscious mad scientist, and this panting man. The doctor had a red mark on his head, and a stab wound in the right side of his chest. Claudia wondered if he was dead, but she couldn't tell.

"We're getting out of here." The man's voice was broken just as hers often was. He grabbed her by the shoulder and tugged them both out of the room and toward the front door. To Claudia's surprise, she fell limp to his grasp.

"Pick up your feet, girl," the man growled at her, "or we're both dying at the hands of that madman. Is that what you want?" Madman… Madman? A spark went off in Claudia's brain. Doctor Cornelious was the madman of which he spoke.

"What'd you do to him?" Her mouth moved in slow motion. She didn't know what was happening to herself. Was she being saved?

"He's out cold for now. Don't know for how long." The man opened the door by a crack and peeked out. "Now where's that mutt?"

"Schnuggles?" The man's face twisted the second Claudia said the name of the creature that so often consoled her.

"That *thing* has a name?" he growled at her. She could only find herself nodding like a buffoon. He shook his head at her, mumbling something about loose screws, and took another peek through the crack in the door.

"Alright, I don't know where it is, but this is our only chance," he explained, while thrusting something in her hands. It was a very large butcher knife, almost the length of Claudia's forearm. There was blood on it, still wet. Her stomach somersaulted as she realized that the man wasn't cut at all. Making a side glance at her, he opened the door a little more, then poked his head out. "The second we start going, just keep running. But we can't ditch each other. We're gonna have to rely on each other to survive. They may come after us, but I have an idea as to where we're going." Claudia nodded numbly, unsure of herself. "Use the knife to protect yourself. That bitch has nothing when it comes to fighting. If he knows your face, he'll pause before attacking you for the kill… That'll be your chance."

Was she really going home? Would she see her friends and family, and continue with a normal life full of normal people? Would they force her into therapy and pity her for going through such a horrible experience? Would she ever carry on normally?

Would she ever be able to leave the doctor?

Before she could make up her mind, the man had grabbed her empty hand and tugged her out of the house, into the dusk. They disappeared into the corn, legs stumbling and running as fast as they could.

Claudia's mind was racing. Leave the doctor? Forever? They'd come so close to knowing each other. She'd gotten so attached to him… to Schnuggles. Her mind was screaming at her to turn back, but her legs were still carrying her away. Tears filled her eyes as she continued to panic like no panic she'd felt before.

And then it hit her.

She stopped suddenly, grasping his hand.

"Wait," she said. He turned to her, exasperated.

"There's no waiting. We have to go NOW, or we're not surviving."

"You don't understand!" Claudia sounded so desperate, but it was all she could do.

"What don't I understand?"

"This."

And the knife was in his chest before he could fight back.

Chapter Nine

The most surprising thing about stabbing someone was how much it *hurt*.

Everything inside of Claudia's being was in pain. Her heart ached, her stomach churned, and her arms burned. Still, she continued to stab the man below her with full vigor. Up and down her arms went, further into the caving rib cage. She would hear the snaps and pops of the bones beneath her breaking. Every sickening crunch she felt with her hands. The grip around the knife stayed tight, her knuckles staining in red. Her thighs were shaking as she slowly lowered herself closer to the body, now sitting on his hips as if straddling a lover. The knife rose and fell, and Claudia was now screaming. Her tears fell toward the body, pooling into the deep gashes she was causing.

The man had stopped making noises some time ago. But she hadn't. Her screams had slowly grown louder and louder, her sobs becoming uncontrollable. Her body shook all over, her muscles tightening more than they had ever before. Every movement pained her and drove her closer to the edge of insanity.

She wouldn't lose him. For the past months, her life in that cabin was all she came to know. In the back of her mind, she had come to enjoy every moment of it. The fear kept her alive. How could she go back to a normal life? Nothing would satisfy her anymore. She would attend church, go to class, work a job, but nothing would keep her happy. It had all grown so dull in her mind. Here, she could do anything. Even kill a man and get away with it.

Her throat felt like it was cutting itself in two as she continued to scream as though her life depended on it. Her eyesight was nothing but globs of color due to the thick tears. Her hands moved on their own, thrusting up and down, back into the chest of the long dead man below her. She was lost inside her own self-pity and the rejoice that she wouldn't have to leave all that mattered to her.

Her mind spun when something grabbed her wrists, *hard*. The knife was snatched from her hands so fast and so carelessly, it sliced into her left wrist. The world turned upside-down as she was thrown down to the ground just to look up and see a doubled-over doctor hovering over her.

"Doctor!" she cried, her hands reaching up to embrace him, but immediately retracted when the doctor scowled at her touch. His eyes... they were so angry. An icy silence hung in the air as the doctor stared mindlessly down at her, bleeding onto her. His wound from earlier hadn't healed. She wondered how long she'd been sitting there, hacking into that man's body.

Time stood still there, in the cornfield.

"Doctor..." she said again, eyes once more filling with hot, sticky tears. The glob on her face, the reek of death that once bothered her, failed to phase her now. Her hair was matted down with blood, guts, and dirt, her entire body disgusting and weak. "I took care of him, see?" Her voice was more desperate than a little child trying to get the attention of a neglecting parent. "I- I took care of him!" Her voice was rising as tears rush down her face, wanting so badly for this entire night to have never happened.

Thunder boomed in the distance, the sprinkle before a downpour began to fall on their bodies. Still, the doctor just stared at her while hunkered over her body.

"Don-don't worry. Schnuggles will eat him just like the rest. There isn't much left, but it's still there!" She continued her desperate babble, although she wondered if she was actually making sense. Her desperate sobs sounded nothing like what she was trying to say to the doctor.

She wanted to crawl into his embrace, to feel the warmth she'd felt so long ago in his arms. The warmth would take all the pain away from her, it would make her feel like everything she'd just done was *worth* it.

"I stopped him! I took care of him! I took care of him!" Her

103

voice was raising more and more until she was merely screaming the same sentence over and over again, desperate for any reaction out of her captor.

The downpour began, and finally, the doctor moved ever so slightly. All that moved were his eyes, which now looked over at the dead body lying beside them. Claudia's mouth shut, but her tears continued their forceful way out of her eyes.

Finally, while gingerly holding his shoulder, he rose and turned toward the cabin, drenched from the rain. The rain pounded down on the two, a little pink puddle forming around the dead body. She rose to her own feet slowly, quietly, wondering if she'd done the right thing, and why the doctor was reacting the way he was.

"We'll take care of the body later." The doctor's voice was, as when he was angry, very low. So low, at first Claudia's didn't think it was him. The only proof was the fact that the doctor's lips moved when the voice came out. The feeling of betrayal washed over Claudia so hard she could have fallen to the ground again. Anger bubbled in the lowest of pits in her stomach; jealousy flared in her heart. Her fists were clenched together so hard the sting of the cut made her wince, but just for a moment.

"Aren't you happy I stopped him?!" she suddenly screamed. His reaction was so alien to her. She hated it. She didn't want this standoffish doctor. She didn't want a normal voice. She didn't want someone who would turn his back to her. She killed this man for one reason and one reason only: To stay the same with Dr. Cornelious.

"I did this for *you*! I did this for us! Goddammit, why can't you just-" She stopped herself when the doctor glanced back at her, his gaze more piercing than she'd ever seen before.

"Us...?" His lower, alien voice continued. "What's an us? There's an us?"

She was dumbfounded. Why else had he kept her here for so long? Did he not want her? Was he completely fine with the fact that she was nearly snatched from his life?

Claudia's knees shook, her tears burst harder, and her heart sunk until she felt sick. Of course, there was an "us." Otherwise, she wouldn't have felt so needed there. She wouldn't have risked her life by killing someone twice her size for this madman standing in front of her.

"Stop it." The word vomit came now. She wasn't even thinking of what she was saying; she was just letting her withered heart speak its mind. "Just fucking stop it! What's an 'us?' Are you- are you fucking kidding me?!" Her sore throat scratched and burned. She wondered if it was bleeding from the excessive strain. "What's an 'us?' What's a fucking 'us!?'"

Her mind snapped; she felt like she was falling, yet her body still stood while vertigo came. Her dirty hair stuck to her face as the rain continued to beat down on her.

"If it weren't for me, cops would be here by tomorrow, and you'd be fucking done for! You'd be dead!" Her heart screamed from her body, her face burning with anger. "DEAD. As in no more Doctor Cornelious! No perfect human. NOTHING. DEAD. FUCK!" Her hands were in her hair, her mind weaving in and out of knowing what to do and not. One side of her was regretting her decision, but the rest of her burned in such anger toward the doctor, if she still had the knife she felt she would run at him with it.

The doctor turned to face her; his head tilted to the side in question as he watched the girl before him. His usual bright blue eyes had a dull haze to them; his manic smile replaced with a deep, deep frown. So deep, she could see lines forming in his face. His pale skin almost looked white to her, and one would wonder if the grays and whites in his hair had increased.

"No." Claudia discontinued her rampage of words when the doctor spoke abruptly to her. She blinked, surprised at his reaction. No? No what?

"I would leave," the doctor continued. "You think... you think this is the first place?" His voice was back. High pitch, squeaky, but in so much pain. The dull in his eyes, Claudia now realized, was the first sign of tears Claudia had ever seen in the doctor before.

"You think I've always been... here?" His words seemed so distant, so forced, like he didn't want to speak of any of this. Like he wanted to forget this night happened. Claudia could not fathom that something could be too much for the doctor to handle. She thought he could tackle anything with a witty remark and a wink, but this doctor, this vulnerable little thing in front of her, she pitied.

"No cops find me. You would go home. You would continue a life... and I would continue mine somewhere else." Her heart hurt at his words. "Schnuggles and I go elsewhere. You forget us through therapy. You continue simple life of disgusting non-perfection." His face was emotionless, his eyes sorrowful. Claudia put a hand over her mouth to force back a sob. Just *hearing* about leaving the doctor for a normal life made her entire body want to crumble.

"No cops find me... Never do."

Claudia couldn't take it anymore. Everything she was feeling, was any of it worth it? All this pain and hurt. Had she ever *really* been happy in this cabin? Or was she just terrified of going back to her old life and the doctor eventually finding her and finishing her off to cover his secrets? With all of her body parts screaming in pain, she approached the doctor slowly. She didn't know what she'd do once she reached him, but she continued her trek. Finally, they were nearly nose-to-nose. Claudia could smell the peppermint thick on the doctor's breath. The tears continued to trickle down her cheeks freely, the chokes of sobs crawling from her throat.

Like a flash of lightning, the sound of skin making contact with skin echoed through the dead corn. Placed prettily against the doctor's face was a bright red, perfect, hand mark. Claudia's hand dropped back to her side limply as she stared at him listlessly, a small amount of contentedness growing in her chest. "So how many other girls were there?" she asked, her croaking voice sounding more determined than before. Claudia felt as though she was having an out-of-body experience. On the inside, she wanted to hug the doctor and scream and cry, be given the attention she'd so desperately wanted from him for so long. But on the outside, her body was just reacting. She felt so weak, but her body stood strong. She wanted to touch the doctor gingerly, but instead she stood very stoic away from him, staring him down in malice.

"What?" The doctor instinctively put a hand on his face as he composed himself, his other hand tightening around the knife. A look of pure confusion plastered across his face. In Claudia's delirium, though, she wasn't having any of it.

"How many?" she growled at him, the burning hatred growing in her heart. "You make me feel like I'm the only one to survive with you, but now the cops never find you? Now you've gone to other towns? How many, dammit! How many women have you done this to! How many Catherine's are there? Do we all just

106

take her name after a while?!" Claudia's hand rose again, but before it made contact with the other side of the doctor's face, he grabbed her by the wrist and threw her down to the ground.

And then Claudia felt it.

The knife was in her arm faster than she'd thought the weakened doctor could react. The pain ebbed into her body, causing the muscles being stabbed to constrict and try to force themselves from her body. But just as quickly as the pain came, it was gone. All she could feel was excessive pressure pushing against the top part of her left arm.

In a haze, Claudia looked from the doctor to where the pressure came from and found the knife sticking out of the inside of her arm. Had the knife moved a few inches to the right, it could have landed a fatal blow to her chest. In a moment of realization and numbing fear, the girl realized just how much danger she had just put herself in. She tried to open her mouth to say something but found herself in such shock that she was unable to mutter a word. Had he just attacked her? The doctor, the man she loved, was he capable of hurting her?

Deep inside Claudia's throat came the sound of a wounded animal. The smell of peppermint mixed with blood made her dizzy. From above her, the doctor was leaning against the knife, his eyes wide and panicking. His mouth was wide open, his breath was heavy, and he stared past Claudia, at the ground, with a blank expression. It wasn't until then that Claudia realized the doctor's entire body was nearly vibrating from shaking so hard. Worry and remorse swept over the estranged girl as she reached up with her free hand to stroke the doctor's face.

He immediately flinched away but seemed to snap out of whatever it was that had shaken him. He blinked down at her, regaining awareness of what exactly he was doing, before taking a big deep breath and regaining his composure. More thunder boomed in the distance, causing Claudia to flinch, deepening the thrust of the blade. She hissed in pain as the doctor leaned back and put one finger up to hush her. She attempted to calm herself the best she could.

"Now... If I wanted you dead, you would be." The doctor's squeak was quiet and unsettling to Claudia. "You would be dead right here and now. Next to this mess you've made." Claudia could only bring herself to nod dumbly at the doctor. "However.

I am not a murderer. A scientist, yes, someone who fails at his experiments..." The doctor paused. "Yes. But not someone who kills for the enjoyment. Unlike you." The last words were venom to Claudia. Leaning in close, the doctor approached her face, the tips of their noses touched. The smell of peppermint gagged her. "I don't kill for the point of killing. My subjects die regrettable deaths during my experiments. But I want them to live. The moment they live, my experiment is a success." A hand, although twitching and nervous to the touch, was brushing Claudia's matted hair away from her face. "The day I succeed in destroying anger and love, while still maintaining personal thoughts and choices in a human mind... No one will kill anyone. Now hold still. This will hurt." The doctor leaned back while putting one hand on her right shoulder, the other grasping the knife tightly. Claudia held her breath as he braced himself against her and pulled the knife back, hard. She took a big gulp of air and panted the second it left her body, and rolled over onto her stomach as the doctor moved away.

Up came the vomit. Up came the extreme pain. All of it together, swirling all around her, enveloping her. The death... the remorse... the depression. It was everywhere. She wished she could force it all from her body just like the fluids coming from her.

But she couldn't. They were all there. And she'd chosen it.

~ ~ ~

They made their way through the storm only with the aid of the other. The pair were forced to lean on the other, stopping every few paces due to the pain one was going through. The trip was slow and agonizing, both of their bodies begging to stop and rest.

When they clambered into the cabin, the two collapsed onto the old dirty couch, tired and defeated. The only sound filling the cabin was their jagged breaths, gasping and begging for an increase of oxygen for their lungs. Claudia wondered if she'd ever felt this much pain in her short life.

To her right was the creator of all her pain, physical, mental, and emotional. She closed her eyes and sat for a moment, attempting to collect her frazzled thoughts. But at the moment, all she could notice was the strong smell of peppermint filling her nose. Without thinking, the deranged girl nuzzled her body toward the madman beside her, smelling the only thing that brought her comfort.

Immediately, the doctor stiffened, and his voice hitched in surprise. But by now, Claudia didn't even notice. The deranged girl was no longer taking mental notes to her surroundings. Everything that had been inside her, all the pain, confusion, love, and curiosity, it was all broken now. All this pain, caused by a single little man, had finally broken her completely. Not even an hour ago, she'd killed a man. She'd refused escape from the harsh reality that was the log cabin. She'd decided that any thoughts were unecessary, because all that mattered was the doctor.

She needed him. Her carnal need for the doctor was tearing out from inside her ribcage. It attacked what little bit of her soul she had left and tore the terrified thing to shreds. The carnal desire would destroy everything to get to the doctor, even if it meant destroying all simple thought and risking Claudia's life.

He mattered so much to her it just caused her more pain. Her poor, delusional mind was losing everything she had once been, and in its place, it was making her into the doctor's pet. She wanted to cry out at just how badly she yearned for the doctor at that moment, the rest of the world melting around her. She felt as though she couldn't breathe until he blew air into her lungs. Why was he so important to her? Did it matter? No. Nothing mattered. Nothing mattered except the doctor.

That smell. The smell of peppermint. It had always been on his breath. It was such a soothing smell. Had it always been there? Yes, it had to be… it was such a soothing quality to the madman. It made him feel so human, so *delicious*.

She was leaning her body into his own as she continued to nuzzle closer into his neck. He was so intoxicating. So addicting. He was the best drug she'd ever tried; he gave her the best high. She smelled him, embracing the peppermint like an old friend.

"Dunce-girl." His voice was nothing but a tiny squeak in his surprise, and Claudia only relished in the sound, her nose now grazing his earlobe, her lips centimeters from touching the skin of his neck. Her head was swimming in peppermint. Everything felt so perfect to her. She was about to touch the one thing that *completed* her.

Her body grew hot as the carnal desire took complete

control over her, scratching, needing, *feeding* the top priority of her life. The cheeks of her face grew scalding hot in flush, the tips of her fingers itched in anticipation, and her lips twitched with a lustful hunger. She pressed her aching body fully into the doctor now, relishing in the feeling of the two being against each other. The time of the heat, the time he held her and called out Catherine's name. That was the day that started her need for him, and it was now at its peak. Now she was drunk with the need for her doctor, and his cold body was molding so well with hers, she felt as though she would die from sheer bliss.

Suddenly, the girl was flung from her comfortable spot against the doctor and was on the ground. Her initial reaction was to how hard she'd been pushed, followed by immense displeasure that she wasn't wrapped in the scent and *being* of Doctor Cornelious. She scrambled as fast as she could to her feet but was stopped dead in her tracks by the sudden realization of excessive pain in her arm. Dizziness filled her mind as she fell back to the ground in a clump. Looking up, she saw the sneer of the doctor standing above her. He hadn't glared at her so angrily since the early days of her stay with him.

No. He wouldn't take this from her. She wouldn't let him.

"Who ARE you?" The doctor was screeching at her now. "This is NOT Claudia."

"Not Claudia? I'm right here!" The desperate shell of a girl screamed at him. "I've been right here this entire time, trying to know what the hell you keep me here for. And… and I'm here! I'm here! You see?" The girl didn't know that she wasn't making any sense. Her blood was too busy boiling in anger. He was going to keep himself away from her. She didn't want to allow it anymore. The doctor was hers and only *hers*. Damned be Catherine, other victims, the police, any being in this existence. She wouldn't let anyone else have him. If he tried keeping himself away… she would stop it. If she had to *kill* him to make it known that he was hers, then so be it. She'd killed once. She'll kill again.

"You can't see anything! So blinded by your pathetic need to make the perfect person; so desperate to make another *Catherine*." She was forcing herself to her feet, despite her legs wobbling and her head swimming.

"Dunce –girl… Claudia. Stop it." The doctor reached to pat her shoulder awkwardly, but instead, the girl swatted his hand

110

away.

"You're *mine*. You're my *perfect being*. You won't make a Catherine because she is pathetic and weak. You made yourself, and you're *mine*."

"I said stop it." His voice was deepening to a dangerous tone, the squeak gone in seconds. But Claudia had passed the point of thinking. Her body was on auto-drive, fueled by a childish hatred and jealousy toward the name Catherine, and the need to have her doctor once and for all.

"Catherine won't come back. But I will. I'm here right now." The babbling coming out of the girl's mouth didn't even make sense. "You say this isn't Claudia. But look at me. I'm Claudia. I'm your Claudia."

"Do *not* speak about her," the doctor demanded, his eyes forming slits as he glared down at her. But Claudia had gone too far to stop.

"Speak of who? Catherine? You're right. We won't speak of old news because we have us now. You don't need that *picture* of her. Let's get rid of it. You have me." Claudia had now turned to walk toward the room that she knew his bedroom was, but before she could so much as take a step, she felt something grab her by the bleeding shoulder and slam her down to the floor.

She hissed in pain as she went down, but was immediately fighting back what was fighting against her. Above, Dr. Cornelious was trying to hold the girl down, all the while also trying to grab hold of her tiny neck to squeeze. In the past, Claudia would have crumbled and allowed the punishment to come, but now she felt *powerful*. Her need to keep what was hers was too powerful to let her just lay down and let it happen. She struggled against him, reaching for his hands to attain the upper hand and flip him over. However, instead, the two found themselves in an awkward position. Claudia had succeeded in grabbing one of the doctor's hands, but he had succeeded in pinning her down to the floor with one of his knees and his other hand. His bone dug into her side. Meanwhile, she was reaching for the knife that had been discarded long ago. The girl reached too slowly, though, as the doctor swiped the knife away with his foot.

"What is WRONG with you?!" he squealed. She merely snarled back at him, taking her hand and going for his still fresh stab wound in his chest. She reached two fingers into the hole, grabbed, and twisted as hard as her little fingers would. The doctor yowled in pain immediately, toppling to the side to try to get away from the hold.

This was her chance. As his body left hers, she rolled toward the butcher knife and took hold of it while rolling onto the balls of her feet and rising in victory. She turned to face the doctor, who was already back on his feet and facing her, a scalpel in his hand. She held the knife like a broadsword, analyzing everything about the madman in front of her.

"You're *mine*, doctor," she hissed at him.

"You're wrong," he merely responded in a low growl. He lunged at her. She turned away from him, lashing out with the butcher knife with all the might she could muster. She heard fabric rip, but before she could react, the doctor was upon her and grabbing her by the shoulders, pushing her as far back as he could.

They were in the fireplace. Claudia screamed out in agony as her back was licked with the familiar pain of the fire, her wet dress only protecting her in the smallest of amounts. Reacting only in her newly found murderous instinct, she reached behind her and grabbed whatever log she could find and swung it between herself and the doctor, directly at his face. The doctor jumped back while protecting his eyes with one of his arms, the log flinging toward the mildew-smelling couch.

It immediately ignited; the tongues of the flames lapped up the old, dusty material like paper. Claudia didn't waste time; she lunged for the doctor, knife still in hand. He uncovered his eyes in time to see the attack and managed to move her hands away with a graze only on his side. The girl screamed in anger, her mind now shut down, all she could think was needing the doctor as hers and only hers.

"Claudia!" She couldn't even hear the doctor over the insanity eating away at her soul. The fire of the couch was spreading now, onto the drapes, down some of the driest of spots on the wooden floor. Still, the two fought.

"Stop it!" The doctor was screaming. Still Claudia was going. She slashed, sliced, and stabbed, missing every time. Grunts and screams were all that came from her mouth as she tried and tried again to lunge into the love of her tormented life.

"If I can't have you, she sure as hell won't!" Claudia was screeching in a frenzy, giving the doctor a chance to grab both her wrists so hard that the girl dropped the knife, but she continued screaming.

In Claudia's first days at the cabin, the doctor was so shocked that she never screamed... yet there Claudia was, screaming as if everything she wanted depended on it.

The doctor took the girl and pinned her against a wall as hard as he could muster, holding tight to her wrists. Behind them, the fire licked up the cottage. Claudia struggled against his hold, her legs kicking whenever they could. Eventually, the madman had her lifted off the ground by her back against a wall and her wrists. She continued to struggle, growling and spitting at the doctor like a rabid animal. She managed to bite him once, causing him to in turn slap her across the face - hard. In letting go and hitting her, Claudia found quick freedom and used the momentum of the slap to run toward the left, deeper into the quickly burning house.

The doctor came fast after her.

She could hear him calling after her, his voice going between a shrill squeal and a low, menacing growl.

She made it into his bedroom and slammed the door behind her before swooping for the little music box that was under the bedside table. When the doctor slammed the door open, his eyes immediately came to the music box.

"....Don't." His voice was deep, deeper than she'd ever heard it before. "Don't you hurt her!" He didn't think, just reacted. He jumped at her with the scalpel, hitting her directly in the thigh. With a quick scream, the girl fell to the floor in sudden pain and the music box toppled to the smoke-drenched floor. Clutching her leg in pain, Claudia immediately tried crawling over to the box, and the doctor stared at her with the look of disgust on his face.

"What became of you, Dunce-girl?" he squeaked as he leaned to grab the box.

He shouldn't have done that.

Claudia immediately took the initiative to remove the scalpel from her thigh and dive for his hand, stabbing it in the middle. The doctor screamed, screamed so loud it echoed off the walls, and the adrenaline-fueled Claudia grabbed the box, found herself on her feet, and limped as fast as she could out of the room, and into an already fire-filled hallway.

The smoke. It choked her, made her blind. She coughed back in retaliation and was about to dive into the hell that was becoming the cabin, but was grabbed from behind and tugged back.

Dr. Cornelious had his arms around the girl's waist, much like the time after her fever, and was tugging her away from the fire.

"Stop! Stop! STOP!" he was repeating shrilly, sounding all too desperate and scared. But she wouldn't listen.

"No!" she yelled back, the roar of the fire drowning most of her voice out.

"Catherine- Catherine I can't lose you again!" he yelled over the fire. Claudia's blood ran cold immediately, and when she turned to slap the man for daring to call her that *name*, she realized he was falling into a much worse delirium than she'd thought possible.

His eyes looked hollow, like holes. The lines on his face made him look older, or perhaps his proper age, and his mouth was quivering in panic.

"Catherine. Don't worry. We'll go find a home…" he cooed to her, trying to pull her toward his operation room, away from the fire. Upon opening the door, though, the two realized that the fire had quickly spread through the walls, and was already engulfing the room. The stench of cooking corpses wafted from the doorway, making Claudia feel sick.

"Stop it! Catherine is gone! GONE. SHE MAY AS WELL BE DEAD." Claudia screamed through her nausea, breaking free from his grasp. She was out the door before she had much time to think, to react. Through more doors she went - ones she barely even recognized. When she came to a halt, it was as though she'd run smack dab into an invisible wall. The stench. Dear god the stench. It was everywhere. With quickly panicking eyes, Claudia took in what was before her. Five bodies. Five of them. Just piled upon the other in the corner of the room. That was it.

All of their eyes were open.

They were all looking at her, with those wide, vacant eyes. And they all were women. Every single one.

All small. All looked to be her age. All women.

All sharing characteristics that she did.

If Claudia wasn't going through complete and utter shock before, she was now. From behind her, through the roar of the fire, she heard the doctor fast approaching.

She *looked* like them.

His footsteps were coming closer.

She *looked* like *them*.

He was calling her name - her real name, not Dunce-girl.

She looked like them.

He was on her, hands grabbing her shoulders from behind, and she found herself wrenching away from him - further into the room that reeked of cooking flesh.

"What... What are these?!" she found herself screaming as she came to her knees in front of the burning pile of bodies. "WHAT ARE THESE?"

"Catherine. Oh, Catherine. It's alright Catherine," he was babbling from behind her, one of his hands was trying to run through her hair but was shaking so uncontrollably it just tugged at it lightly. "Just give me back Catherine. Catherine. Oh, Catherine."

"Shut it!" Claudia was trying to form a coherent thought besides the one repeating in her head. They looked like her. Why? Why did they look like her? One looked like it'd been rotting there, on the bottom of the pile, for some time. Some of the skin had already begun to rot away. Had Claudia grown so familiar with the smell of death that she never noticed it - being in the same building as the monstrosity in front of her?

"They... I look like them! Why do I look like them? I thought I wasn't an experiment... Doctor!" The madman continued to blow from behind her, making the occasional swipe for the box in her hands. However, the girl held strong to it.

"Doctor!" she screamed over the roar of the flames. She turned to look back at him, finding his hands in his face - unable to deal with the situation at hand, she supposed.

"*Tell me!*" she screamed, her voice echoing off the shambling walls in heartbreak.

"Nononono... Not like them. Not like them. You - you look like *her*... and they look like *you*... But you. You're the middle. You're the middle." The doctor was speaking so quickly she almost couldn't follow him. "You're the middle, you see? Now give... give Catherine back. Please. Catherine..."

"So that's it? That's been it all along?" Thunder boomed over the sound of the fire licking up their home. The hiss of water meeting fire filled her ears. "All this time... All this time I thought. I don't know what I thought. I thought I was yours. I thought -" and suddenly with one swift movement, Claudia threw the little music box into the fire of the room, watching as the doctor's expression went from desperation... to blank.

As if the music box itself had been what had possessed Claudia into her delirium, the girl came to a sudden realization of what she'd just done, to not only Dr. Cornelious, but to herself.

A weight on her chest was suddenly lifted, and although she was stuck in the middle of a burning log cabin, she felt that for the first time in a long time, she could breathe again. With new eyes, she took in her surroundings, and felt terrified. Her body felt as though it could no longer hold itself up, as she fell to the floor and felt all the pain and wounds she'd caused herself in the last few hours. Her eyes filled up with immediate tears of regret, and she wondered who exactly she was.

The doctor had been right. She wasn't her. And it took a simple music box being engulfed in flames to make herself realize that. What had caused her to lose all of her sanity? What had made her feel that killing the doctor would keep him near her? Guilt and remorse flooded her body. The mental sickness... It all made her head swim. Everything was so wrong. She shouldn't care for the doctor. The doctor shouldn't have even kept her alive. He should have experimented on her and called it a day. But there they were, both bloodied and full of holes because they drove each other to the brink of insanity.

She felt so defeated at this moment as her head lolled to the ground while her body crumpled to the floor. Everything was growing hazy now. The want to lose consciousness and die from blood loss filled the girl's heart as she realized she was the fault of almost everything that was happening here. She was never strong willed; she never had the ability to hold herself high. Instead, she succumbed to deliriums and murder. And she took the doctor down with her.

The thought that she would finally die filled her mind, and although she was partially relieved, she was also filled with extreme fear. She felt around for something and felt a scalding hold gurney beside her which she used to hoist the top of her body up.

And that's when she saw it...

His eyes were like holes deep inside his head, never seeing, yet searching the entire room. It was as though all color had left them, revealing that all the humanity left within his soul had

116

finally snapped and died. His brown and white hair was matted down with gobs of blood and guts, to the point that some of it was plastered on his face like melted plastic.

Claudia Boswell felt sick as she inhaled the stench of rotting corpses. As she tried to lift her hand to cover her mouth to hold in whatever contents remained in her stomach, she noticed the blood on her hand, only causing her to feel even sicker. Her body lurched as she fought to maintain her composure.

The doctor turned to look over at her, causing her skin to turn to ice. Was this all real?

"Doc-" Opening her mouth proved to be a bad idea for Claudia. She kneeled down onto her knees, facing the ground until her body stopped lurching and she could breathe again. Instead of immediately standing, she sat, staring down at her own waste. To her, it was better than the nightmare she was now in.

The stench of burning bodies still overpowered her. It was a thick smoke, wrapping itself around her whole body; getting into her hair, her clothes, under her fingernails. Her eyes welled up from the entire predicament engulfing her, and she coughed back the temptation to cry.

Dr. Cornelious continued to stare at her, the holes in his head giving no sympathy, or even recognition that the man she'd come to know was still there. His body was rigid, stuck in the slumped-over position he'd twisted himself into. Without straightening his body, he took a step toward her. It looked almost like he was limping rather than walking, or even gliding.

Out of the corner of her eye, Claudia saw him come toward her. In reflex, she scooted herself away from him. She fought up the nerve to look up at his shoes, but couldn't bring herself to stare into those maddened eyes. There was a moment of silence, the two staying very still. Claudia's mind was buzzing with screams of agony and fear. She didn't know if saying anything would have fixed anything, or for the matter, saved her life.

She was going to die. She was going to die by the hands of someone she'd come to *trust*. Feeling dizzy, she attempted to gather her senses and squirm her way until she felt a wall against her back. Once there she pushed herself against it and forced her feet up to aid her to stand. Her legs were weak; her knees shook uncontrollably.

The sound of a grunt made her panicked eyes immediately

shoot up, only to find the horrors of Doctor Cornelious slowly approaching her, dragging his cleaver with mild discomfort. His knuckles were white with how hard he was holding onto the weapon, and his eyes were wide with madness. His lips curled into a sick smile, and his feet nearly stumbled over one another as he slowly limped his way over to her.

Claudia couldn't help but let out the sobs she'd been holding back this whole time. Tears quickly ran down her cheeks and muffled whimpers crawled out of her throat. Her mouth felt like it'd been filled with cotton balls as she tried to open it and form more words, but her tongue acted as though it swelled, and she found nothing to come out but more chokes and whimpers.

She stared down at the floor, her mind racing in circles as to what to do. The only thing in her mind was how to survive. How would she? What would she do?

By now her thick tears had formed lines down her dirty face, little pink droplets fell from her pointed chin down to the floor. Her eyes flicked down to the droplets, watching them mix with a falling stream of gooey, red liquid. She tilted her head in wonder at this liquid. She knew very well it was blood, but whose was it? And why was it so close to her?

Her eyes traced the blood, following the falling droplet's up past her body to see none other than the menacing Dr. Cornelious standing above her. His lips were peeled back in a menacing grin; his bright white teeth clenched together in an annoyed fashion. His breath was now blowing down onto her face, those black holes of eyes stabbing into her soul and making her wish she was already dead.

Then it came out. Something Claudia didn't even think of before it happened. It was as though the question was alive, and wanted to come out on its own for closure. Her lips parted, and it raced out into the face of its victim, full of bitterness and hatred.

"WHY?" Her voice sounded almost alien. She thought that it would be the one thing that would end it all, so her eyes clenched shut and she braced herself for the cleaver to come down on her.

Instead, the doctor's smile slowly faded. His wide, empty eyes continued to stare down at her as the fist that held so dearly to his cleaver began to tremble. His lips formed a trembling frown; his eyes pooled up with tears. His breath became shaky, and sounded like he was struggling just to breathe on his own.

Finally, he let out one quick scream as he lifted the hatchet and brought it down upon her.

Chapter Ten

There was a loud *thunk* as the hatchet slammed into the wall behind Claudia as her breath hitched in fear. Splinters of wood flew past her face as her panicked eyes flicked about, trying to process her situation.

She was alive. That much she could tell. She felt a faint prick from her right ear, followed by numbness that spread across that entire side of her face. She wondered if he'd lopped off the entire thing and her body was reacting to protect itself. But that didn't matter much at the moment. What mattered was the man standing above her, the one whose breath she could feel on her face.

Peppermint. Always *peppermint.*

She made eye contact with him and realized immediately how much of a mistake that was. His icy eyes were almost pulsating, staring, unblinking back at her. His pupils were so small, barely illuminated by the brightness of his irises. The black holes were gone, and in place shone the sunken eyes of an empty man. His breathing came in ragged, irregular gasps, and his body limped toward her, leaning on the hatchet for support. The blue in his eyes, rather than icy, was glossed over; the madman was about to cry out and turn to what he once was.

The thought to speak crossed the rattled mind of Claudia Boswell, but she found she was unable to do so. She couldn't do much of anything except stare. Even breathing proved to be a difficult task. After all, these horrible breaths could be her last, yet she found herself wondering if she cared. After all she'd been through in that small cabin, did it matter if her end was near?

Without thinking, Claudia reached up toward the lunatic before her and rested a hand on his cheek. There was a quick flinch before his entire body stiffened. They sat like that, minutes rolling by, both almost holding their breath.

Claudia forgot how to breathe again when she felt the pressure of a large hand pressed against her face as he slammed her head into the wall behind her. All she could hear was the screaming of intangible words and sobbing. She didn't realize the sobbing was her own until she felt the damp of the doctor's hand push harder onto her face, smothering the woman in her tears. But the screaming… was Dr. Cornelious.

This was his breaking point, and she'd caused it to happen.

Her hands scrambled against him, one grabbing his hair, the other trying to pry him off of her. Her mind, although distorted not even minutes earlier, was so clear; she not only feared him, she feared herself. She needed away from this horrible mess; she needed salvation. However, dying in that cabin by burning alive was not how she wanted to go.

She tried speaking, but was only met with more force from the hand that held her. She wondered what would happen first, her skull crushing in or the wall giving way. She didn't get to figure it out, though, as suddenly the hand let go of her, and she heard the doctor screaming in surprised agony. As her vision cleared, she saw that one of his pant legs had caught fire. Without hesitation, she leaped for his leg and began patting it out with her hands, the fire licking up her flesh as she hissed in agony. The doctor was writhing, panicked and confused, as she grabbed his shoulders and forced him to face her.

"We need to get out of here!" she screamed over the roar of the flames, which had quickly grown to engulf half of the old cottage already. The doorway, their only escape, was all but consumed in a wall of fire. From beyond the wall, she could hear the panicked howl of none other than Schnuggles, likely back from wherever he'd been and unknowing as to what to do.

"Stay back Schnuggles!" the crazed doctor yelled, despite the animal likely not hearing him. "Stay back! Back!" He staggered toward where the front door once was, as the ceiling above him gave way. Claudia didn't think, she simply acted. Before she knew it, she was ramming the doctor in the waist, and they were both

121

thrown against a weak wall that was doused in flames. Behind them, the collapsing ceiling landed around what had once been their living room, and smoke was enveloping their entire space from the rain meeting the fire.

The doctor screamed in pain as the fire laced up his clothing. She pulled him back, once more patting him down until he grabbed her wrists and tugged her toward the section of the cottage that wasn't quite engulfed in flames yet.

"We can climb through the window in the lab!" the doctor yelled over the roar of the flames, "don't breathe the smoke!" But Claudia was already finding it very hard to breathe, her breath spurting in coughs. He nearly dragged the girl down the hallway and into the lab. But when the door was thrust open, they were met with more fire and the stench of burning corpses. Claudia, overtaken by the smell, gasped, and was met with more fire licking its way down her throat. Before she could react, the doctor stuffed a wad of his shirt over her mouth.

"Stop it!" he screeched as he dragged her by the arm toward his bedroom. He opened the door with a stiff kick, and they found this room, although filled with smoke, easier to navigate. The two scrambled toward the window, when suddenly, Doctor Cornelious's attention was taken from him.

"Wait!" he said, backtracking toward the dresser in the corner of the room. Claudia pulled back.

"We don't have time!"

"I need the box!" he responded before her, "I *need* it."

"You won't need it if you're dead!" Claudia shot back. But it fell on deaf ears as the doctor detached himself and sprinted for the old wardrobe. Rather than argue, Claudia began trying to open the windows. However, in thought, she realized that opening them would likely cause a change in pressure, causing the fire to spread faster, and hit them as they were trying to escape. She needed the doctor, and they needed to sprint out of that thing as fast as they could.

"Doctor! I need you," she called, smoke filling her lungs as they tried to expel it through painful coughing. Nothing. She turned to see the room full of smoke; she couldn't even see a few inches before her, much less across the room. "Doctor!" she called again, but once more, nothing. Panic inched up her spine, but before she would call more, she delved into the smoke, both hands reaching out to feel for the madman. She couldn't have moved more than a few steps before she felt his hair in her hands, and she grabbed and yanked. The doctor, likely taken by surprised to be led by his hair, yelped in pain.

"Wait!" he shrieked, "I haven't grabbed it all!"

"You can't take it all! Catherine is *dead*, doctor; you need to accept that!"

"And who says she's dead!?" the doctor exclaimed. "Maybe she's waiting for me - for these clothes! Maybe she's waiting!"

"Doctor Cornelious!" Claudia screamed exasperatedly. The smoke was making her eyes burn, she was losing her strength, and they didn't have much longer. "We need to leave... NOW. Or you will DIE, and if she is still around, you'll never see her again. WE HAVE TO GO." She had turned to face him, both hands on each shoulder, trying to convey her message to the blockheaded man before her.

"But-"

"But nothing, we have to get out!" she exclaimed, pulling him toward her and the window.

They were running out of time, fast, and his dawdling was costing them too much. He fought for a few seconds until Claudia stumbled over her own feet and fell to her knees. That seemed to be enough for him as his appearance changed from panicked to a man with a plan, as he grabbed her good arm and wrapped it around his neck.

"We're jumping through," he said to her hollowly, and before she could react, he was launching the two of them toward the window.

With the explosion of windows shattering and what felt like the fire angrily chasing after them, the two landed in the pouring rain outside, on top of shards of broken glass. Within seconds, the creature Schnuggles was upon them. Claudia couldn't hear much; her body was finally shutting down after dealing with so much in a single day. She could faintly hear the doctor telling her to keep conscious, and before she succumbed to the darkness she whispered-

"I'm sorry."

Chapter Eleven

The repeated sound of beeping filled Claudia's ears as she regained consciousness. The tips of her fingers prickled uncomfortably as she twitched in place, her body feeling stiff and not-of-her-own. She had to will herself simply to open her eyes, and when she did she felt her entire stomach drop to her toes.

She was surrounded by white walls. A little plastic bedside table sat to her immediate left, vases of bouquets crowding the surface. Through the foliage, she spotted a window that framed what looked to be an overcast sky above a bustling city. Her stomach in knots, she hoisted herself to a sitting position, ignoring the painful warnings her muscles were sending her.

Where was she?

"Doctor?" she found herself calling out. In the corner of her eye, she saw a white lab coat flutter past an open door, causing her heart rate to quicken. "Doctor!"

She called louder now, the repeating beep quickening in her ears. Although her deranged mind expected none other than Doctor Cornelious's face to appear in her doorway, a woman in a lab coat sauntered in instead.

"Ah - you're awake!" the woman exclaimed happily.

The taste of bile rose in her throat as she contorted her mouth into a frown at the woman before her. Seeing someone in such a garb who wasn't Doctor Cornelious was damn near a sin to the girl. How dare the woman wear that in front of her, how dare she make Claudia think that her doctor was alive and well.

But wait - was he?

"Where's the doctor?" she suddenly demanded. "Where is he?" She motioned to swing her legs to the side of the bed, but found the woman at her side in lightning-quick speed, trying to push her gently back to a lying position. "I will be your doctor for tonight... Please relax. I know you're probably very confused and scared right now. But don't worry, it's all over now. You're safe." Although her voice should have sounded soft and comforting, Claudia only heard lies.

"You're not that doctor," she breathed, the familiar panic of desperation already masking her voice. "You're - you're not him. Where's the doctor? Where am I?"

"Please, calm down. Like I said, you're safe. Do you want to see your family?"

"I WANT to see the doctor!" Claudia howled at the incompetent woman before her. "Get your hands off of me! Where is the doctor? Doctor?! Doctor!" She was screaming now, trying to push against the false doctor before her, swinging her legs over the bed again. "Doctor where are you?" Her mind was quickly growing hazy in bewilderment as she tried pushing against the woman. However, this stranger was much stronger than Claudia and was easily able to hold her down to the bed.

"Nurse- I need help in here!" the fake doctor called from behind her shoulder. Claudia's panic worsened as she fought back. For a moment, she bit into the woman's dark skin until she tasted copper on the tip of her tongue. The doctor screamed in pain, but more arms were on Claudia, pulling her mouth away from her predator's flesh.

Who were these people, and what had they done to Doctor Cornelious? She struggled against them fruitlessly, flailing both her arms and legs. Voices were trying to calm her in her hysteria for the man that she craved. She couldn't count how many of them were there, all holding her down. In the corner of her eye, she could see someone pull a needle from a box.

"No!" she wailed, "No - I took care of him! I took care of him he can't leave me! He can't!" Her voice sounded foreign even to herself in her desperation. But even as much as she struggled against all these strangers, the prick of the needle met the skin on her neck, and she found herself falling into a darkness that only ebbed at her the more she tried to fight it.

~ ~ ~

Four days, five hours, twenty-two minutes. Time didn't fly by or stand still. It moved at a constant pace. Claudia stared at the digital numbers on her hospital room nightstand, eyes swollen from bouts of sobbing and rubbing. She'd been aware of her surroundings for that long, and she continued to watch the clock, waiting for the impossible to happen.

People had been visiting her in these days: her parents, Becca and Hannah, even Matt had stopped by and left her a bouquet of flowers, a letter attached that spewed some bullshit about how he was so glad she was back and he'd be ready to talk whenever she'd need it.

Lies. It was all lies. Although they all spoke to her often, trying to sound upbeat despite the hitch in all of their throats, trying to sound so happy that she was back in their lives, Claudia knew they were dirty, disgusting liars. They would put on a pretty face for her, one they thought she'd prefer, but it just looked like a mask to her. The first two days she would scrunch her nose at them and never respond, but that would make them lie even more. They'd spew lies about how important she was to them, how their lives were so different without her.

Disgusting, pathetic people. Nowhere near perfect. Only good for giving to the doctor. Only good on a lab table.

They didn't know true happiness, found only in knowing precisely where one belongs. She knew; she belonged at the side of Doctor Cornelious. She belonged in the cabin, in keeping him company on his loneliest of nights. She belonged in being his dunce. His C-named-girl.

She belonged in his fireplace when he was angry, and at the tip of his scalpel when he needed to blow off steam.

And yet these people would insist that she was back where she belonged. She'd snort at them, glare; occasionally she'd altogether stop listening and look out the window. They'd yammer on with their belong bullshit and lies of a supposed fulfilling life in the city that awaited her with them.

Becca and Hannah would try to talk to her like they had before, vomiting up words like a plague. Telling her lie after lie, telling her how they'd changed.

126

But they hadn't.

Becca was a lost cause.

Hannah… she had hope for Hannah. If only she'd give herself to her husband in the way Claudia had. The proper way. The right way. Claudia almost admired Hannah with her commitment to her husband. Almost.

Hilarious. Before, she thought Becca was so exciting; she strived to be like Becca. Hannah had been the boring one, the average one. But wasn't it the opposite? Hannah had always been the closest to understanding true happiness.

Claudia even gave a small smile to Hannah that morning four days, five hours, and twenty-five minutes after she'd awoken. She reached out to touch the drab, straight bob of hair her friend still wore to this day, and lightly tugged a strand.

"He hasn't cut yours… That's nice. You don't cry at night, do you? I did. I was wrong..." Claudia said with a quiet giggle. The other two women stopped their talking immediately and stared at her. Becca was about to open her mouth, but Hannah, always the peacekeeper, held up her finger to hush her.

"…What do you mean, sweetie?" Hannah's voice was like honey in the air. It was smooth and sugary, something that made Claudia's teeth hurt. She ached for the ear piercing sound of the doctor's cackle.

Claudia quietly reached for her hair, still uneven from the amateur cut the doctor had given her many moons before. Although now her hair was clean and didn't reek of death, it was still the uneven perfection the doctor had bestowed upon her.

"The doctor cut mine. I cried that it smelled like the corpses and… and he cut it. But that's okay. I like it like this. He gave it to me." Her voice left her before she could decide if she really wanted to say anything… but these people - these *things* … They should know the greatness that was the doctor, should they not?

The two women exchanged worried glances with one another. Becca clamped her mouth shut awkwardly.

Coward. It was all Claudia could think.

"Sweetie… what are you talking about?" Hannah said to her, "what doctor?"

"Mine. Or should I say I am his? I cannot own him. Catherine gets that honor." The bitterness in Claudia's tone in mentioning Catherine could have cut through the air.

"You're not making sense, Claudia..." Becca tried, earning herself a quick glare from Claudia.

"I don't need to make sense to people like you," Claudia spat, "you don't know love."

"What?" Becca's mouth gaped open like a fish. Hannah just continued to lay Claudia comfortably against her pillows.

"Maybe we should visit another time... you seem upset," the calmer of the three tried, tucking blankets under Claudia's body. "You need time to recover. We understand. We're here for you, hun."

And they left her.

As they left, Claudia realized that she was empty, completely and utterly. Her freedom brought her the racking realization that she would never see Doctor Cornelious ever again, causing words to come out of her mouth she thought she'd never think before. What had she been thinking? She spoke to them about the doctor as if she worshiped him... and Love?

Love. Doctor Cornelious.

There would never again be nights in the rain, standing under it and hoping the stench of rotting corpses would peel off their bodies. There would be no silent nights in front of the fire, the doctor going over notes while Claudia sat and watched him silently. How silly she felt now, having taken those nights for granted. To think she once thought of trying to escape on her own will, or worse, killing him herself. But now she looked on the memories fondly.

It took this much for someone to love him. It took breaking her down and reforming her into a doll. In Claudia's mind, it was the most romantic thing she'd ever witnessed. However, to any other person, they would say it was anything but love. It was sick and wrong.

She didn't care.

Her mood would worsen late into the night, when all of her depression, her rage, and her desperation would finally bubble out of her in fits of screaming, sobbing, and thrashing. Often the nurses would arrive to restrain her, however by then she'd already done her damage. She would punch holes in the wall, throw vases across the room, rip her sheets and pillows. The next morning she'd find herself strapped in harnesses until her mother arrived, who would create such a fuss the doctor would untie her just to make the woman shut up.

Claudia found it ridiculous how, even in the medical world, sometimes the customer is still always right.

Seven days, three hours, twenty-three minutes. If time had changed at all, it would be that it has slowed painstakingly down. Claudia heaved a small sigh, eliciting her mother to pop her head up from her seat like a meerkat. Her mother's eyes stared worriedly at Claudia. She was obviously growing tired with her daughter's condition, and sick with worry. However, Claudia wouldn't give her mother the joy of response, not today. She turned her head to the right and began gazing out the window, small tufts of hair falling just to the tops of her eyes. She blew them away, tilting her head so that her cheek would touch the windowsill, eyes glazing over the scenery.

City. No corn fields. No wildlife.

No Schnuggles.

Claudia's heart wrenched in her chest, her eyes filling with a new batch of tears. Crying was all she was good at these days. Even back at the cabin, all she did was cry. But she didn't care; she had nothing else to do. No one else to impress. Nothing.

"Would you like a shower, love?" the brogue voice of her father came from behind her shoulder. Ah, her parents. Such sweet people, although dull. She never found them dull before, but she did now. Her father, a Scottish-American immigrant, her mother a Georgia peach pageant queen. In the past, she'd found their relationship romantic. Now it left bile in her mouth.

Normalcy. She was destined for it now.

"Don't push her, dear," her mother whispered. "She'll... she'll shower when she's ready. And she'll come back to us when she's ready... Right, Claudia? You'll come back." The hitch in her throat was so pertinent that the woman's words were lost on her.

"Love, go and get yerself' some tea." Claudia's father's voice was low, warm, and soothing. The exact opposite to Doctor Cornelious. It caused Claudia's fingers to twitch in aggravation.

With a few sniffs and a pat on Claudia's shoulder, the soft pitter patter of her mother's footsteps left the room. Then silence. Claudia knew her father was still with her. However, her attention remained on the window, on the horizon.

"So... How about t'day?" she heard him ask.

Claudia said nothing but continued staring.

Seven days, three hours, twenty-six minutes.

A sigh came from behind her head.

"Yer mum's real worried y'know," her father almost cooed to her. "We all thought... we all thought we'd lost ya, Claud." A lump formed in her throat. Claud. Clod. Dunce-girl.

"We're just so happy you're alive... I want -- we want yeh to get bett'r."

"There is no getting better from stupidity," the doctor would say. And he would pet her head, squeak out another Dunce-girl, and leave her at whatever task with which she had been occupying herself.

The tears made their way down her face. Where was he? Was he safe? And Schnuggles?

"William!" The sudden exclamation from the doorway even got Claudia to jump and turn to see what had happened. There in the doorway, no food in hand, stood her mother - frail and frenzied looking. "William! They think they've got him!"

It was all that needed to be said, all Claudia needed to hear. Before either parent could react to their daughter's sudden action, she was up and pushed past her mother in record speeds, running in any direction that seemed correct. She felt tears in both arms, and a racing pain shot up her body. She had forgotten to grab her IVs.

She didn't get far, when before she knew it a hulking man of a nurse was on her, holding her solidly on the ground while she flailed her body with the most strength she felt she'd had in a long time. The shrill screams of a desperate woman filled the halls, calling for a doctor over and over again. It wasn't until her mother and father were near, asking her to calm down through chokes and sobs that she realized it was her screaming, calling for Doctor Cornelious.

The nurse let her flail and scream, her eyes blinded with tears and her throat burning.

But if he was here, if they "had him." No. She couldn't bear even the thought.

She continued to scream until her body betrayed her, and she could scream no more. They had carried her out of the hallway and into another room, which she hadn't even noticed in her frenzy. Through the window that led into the hallway, she could see her parents looking on, her father the look of nothing but saddened support and her mother broken down into his arms.

Claudia didn't care. They didn't matter. The doctors didn't matter. Nothing mattered. Nothing but Doctor Cornelious.

She tried calling for him one last time but found that her throat, now filled with what felt like razor blades and needles, would not allow it. Her voice was nothing but the whisper of a choked mouse. Her tears continued to fall, now onto the bed that they'd so graciously strapped her to. Any flailing she attempted was met with burning skin, sore muscles, and tight restraints.

They had him. They had him, and there was nothing she could do about it.

She continued to call for him, over and over, even with her destroyed voice. It wasn't until the nurses injected her with some sort of needle that darkness began taking her, and she just couldn't bring herself to call for him anymore.

Chapter Twelve

It was all over the news: Tales of a madman who kept a single girl hostage for two years. Claudia heard the reports over and over, all telling the same story but each with a new light. Sometimes they would show pictures of her, of course from before her enlightenment of the doctor. The screens paraded photos of a younger, much more naive Claudia Boswell, hair pinned back in a bun and a smile on her face.

They say she was gone for two years. Two years of her family searching, then giving up, then mourning her death. They had finally begun to heal when the wound was reopened. They found her, destroyed physically and sick in the head.

Claudia had yet to speak with the press. She didn't feel the need to. Every time the lights and the cameras were shoved in her direction, she immediately felt sick to her stomach. Her family protected her, her mother shielding her face with a hat, her father protecting her from the vultures with his arms. When she was allowed to leave the hospital, the press had a field day trying to catch a glimpse of her.

She hated them. Every single one of them. She would keep the windows shut tight day in and day out, worried that the vultures would come for her. Even after they'd long forgotten about her, Claudia continued to hole herself in her parent's house, living numbly and quietly. She found herself within her mind, daydreaming. She found familiarity in the feeling of loneliness. Often she'd find herself thinking that she heard the familiar gruff of Schnuggles or the cackle of the doctor in the distance... But she'd always find nothing, and she was left in her solitude.

If time stood still in the cabin surrounded by dead corn and ran smoothly in the hospital, it passed without grace while back in the real world. Hours would all but disappear to her as she stared longingly out her bedroom window, and days would pass by without her even giving them any realization. If her parents didn't continue to dote on her, she would probably not even notice mealtimes passing and distant relatives coming and going.

One morning, Claudia didn't know which, a soft knock came from her open door, and she looked to find her mother smiling back at her lightly. Her mother had aged exponentially in the past two years - her crow's feet buried deep in the lids of her eyes and wrinkles forming bags wherever they felt fit. Once a beautiful woman, she was now a destroyed mess. Claudia wondered if she looked any better. She assumed that she probably looked worse. She had never been a looker like her mother, so she had a shorter distance to fall from grace.

"A friend from college is here to see you..." her mother's voice was just above a whisper - cracked, quiet, and delicate. Her voice portrayed a woman who suffered through far too much in far too little time. Claudia blankly stared at her mother, not knowing what to say.

"I thought everyone had visited," she flatlined. Her mother's mouth made a sad, thin line across her face. Worry and disappointment painted her features.

"He seemed very adamant in seeing you," her mother tried again. Claudia knew her expression wasn't changing, and it only caused her mother to worry more. People should want to see their loved ones after a traumatic experience, not resent every single one. But how could the girl? They were all so... defective. Like broken toys stuffed in the clearance aisle at a run-down store.

"Oh?" Claudia tried to look intrigued, but her face contorted uncomfortably. Her mother's arms folded below her chest apprehensively.

"Should I tell him to try another time?" the woman tried. Claudia glanced at herself in her vanity's mirror. She stared at her unruly, unkempt hair, still uneven from the scalpel job the doctor had given her some time ago. Her mother had insisted on her cutting it, which had resulted in her biting her poor father's hand when he agreed a hair cutting would do her some good. It was not a high point in her life, but honestly, the horrid and unkempt hair-job was all she had left of the doctor. Her face was pale, her eyes sunken and the shadows from lack of sleep had lightened, but remained. She looked like a ghost woman from the old drowning stories. She glanced back at her porcelain mother.

"Did he say a name?" she asked.

Her mother stared at her quietly, likely annoyed with the fact that Claudia had been avoiding all her questions since she knocked.

"I forgot to ask for it…" she finally said. "Would you like me to go and check?"

"No," Claudia said quietly, almost shortly. She hadn't meant it in any rude or nasty way; she simply didn't want to see her mother look so awkward in her doorway anymore. Perhaps being quick to speak would make her walk away faster.

It didn't.

With a small sigh, Claudia rose onto her sore legs and stretched slowly in front of the vanity, examining the woman before her with mild interest. Where before there had been an all around casual girl - not too pretty and not too ugly - now stood an anorexic skeleton of a person. Skin hugged bones too closely in her arms, her cheeks sunken, causing deeper shadows than she believed should be there. Hollow, empty, missing. All those words could describe her physical looks.

And she knew it.

But her body may as well reflect how she felt on the inside.

She heaved more air out of her nose as she glanced at the older woman in the doorway, still waiting, still watching. She wanted to roll her eyes and make a quip, but already she felt too tired to do that even. With another moment to steal a glance at herself, she silently strode past the woman in the doorway and down the familiar hall of her house. The walls were lined with old family portraits, a smiling toddler, a little girl riding a bike the first time, first days of school. They only made her stomach turn in looking at them.

In the front doorway stood a man Claudia couldn't quite recognize. His skin was olive with the darkest hair she'd ever laid eyes on. His smile was lopsided, as though he was hiding a secret that was the most amusing joke he'd ever heard. When his eyes locked onto hers, Claudia felt her breath catch in her throat.

Icy blue. Terrifyingly blue. So blue they took away her very soul.

She'd only seen one man with eyes that looked like that.

With three long strides, he was upon her, both hands wrapping tightly around the tops of her arms, all while maintaining eye contact with her.

Up close, she saw his eyebrows didn't match. One was white, the other the dark color of the rest of his head.

She opened her mouth to say something to him, to express the loss that she felt with every day that passed without him. But now with all these things bubbling up inside her, she found she couldn't find words. There were too many things she wanted to say, and she wanted to say them all at once.

He shushed her then, putting one finger over her lips. Her whole body shuddered at his gentle touch, and she closed her eyes to savor and memorize the exact feeling. It was as though a simple brush of his finger to her lips was shooting electricity through her. It was more intense than any kiss she'd come to have in her short, meaningless life.

"Oh Dunce-girl…" she heard him murmur.

Her eyes darted open again to meet his, her mouth once more open to speak. She knew his voice. That was his. It was his voice, and it rang in her ears like a bell. The coldness in his blue eyes seemed to soften as he removed his finger from her lips and put it to his, signifying to quiet herself.

She watched. She watched as this man, who somehow wasn't her doctor and yet was, took this same hand and reached into a pocket inside his jacket, before forcing something into her clammy, trembling hands. Claudia merely continued to stare, disbelief growing inside her. It had to be him. It had to. But explain the hair? The skin? He was him, yet he was not.

But they had gotten him, hadn't they?

He moved forward, his lips near her ear as though he wanted to whisper something more to her. His now free hand found both of hers and clasped them together with utmost importance. In his squeeze, she felt paper in her palm, crinkled. Why had he given her paper? What was on it? A note, perhaps?

For a third time, Claudia tried to speak to him. But again her own body betrayed her as she felt tears of happiness well up in her eyes and her throat squeeze in trying not to choke herself in sobs. She could hear her heart pounding so loudly she wondered if he could hear it too in their proximity.

The last time they'd been this close, he thought she was Catherine.

But now he'd called her Dunce-girl. He'd called her the right name.

He knew who she was.

They stood like that, eye-to-eye, him clutching her hands as though both of their lives depended on it. She wanted to stay like that with him, for the rest of time. All her hollowness, all her emptiness; it was now gone. Her everything was with her once more.

And then -

And then nothing.

She was alone.

Claudia blinked back the darkness a few times to realize what had just happened. She wasn't in the living room, standing before a man who was not yet was the mad scientist she'd come to love. She was in her room, in bed, gasping for air as though she hadn't been breathing moments before.

A quick glance around herself made her realize with immense sorrow what had happened.

It had all been a dream.

Damp from sweat and the tears immediately falling from her eyes, Claudia let out a sudden wail of staggering disappointment. None of it had been real. There was no doctor with a new face; he hadn't come to find her. It was all fake.

Before she could so much as take another breath for more of her wails, both her father and her mother were through the door, her mother cradling her like a child and her father inspecting the room as though a monster would jump out and gobble them up at any moment. Claudia only continued to sob, her cries bouncing off the walls and causing her ears to hurt. She'd been so close. He felt like he was right there... And he wasn't. Her mind was now playing tricks on her.

"It's alright baby... it's alright," her mother was crooning as her father approached her window.

"Did y' leave the window open? It's freezin' in here," she could hear her father respond, followed by the sound of the

136

window sliding shut.

"What? No, it was supposed to rain tonight, of course I didn't," her mother murmured back, the exhaustion present even in the real mom, just like dream mom. She patted Claudia's hand, trying to soothe the grown girl out of her stupor - and that was when she felt it.

The prick of the edge of paper crinkled in her hand.

Claudia's cries stopped nearly immediately as she gripped her fist tighter, trying to still her breath as she laid her head in the crook of her mother's neck.

She felt paper.

Wadded paper.

She refused to open her hand, suddenly afraid that her parents would take away something that would be all she had to hold onto.

"Am I dreaming?" she found herself asking as her eyes widened.

"Dreaming? No... no honey. You're really here. You're wit' us," her father tried to comfort her as she felt his weight slowly come down on the bed to her left. "You're safe."

"Safe," she repeated the word, although she didn't feel it. She didn't want the safety of this household; she wanted to know if there was really something in her hand - and that maybe... just maybe...

"Sweetie, your fist is turning white. What's that you've got there?"

"Nothing," she found herself parting from her mother as though the woman burned her. "Nothing. Nothing." Both parents looked very alarmed and ill-equipped to deal with her at this moment.

"Are you sure it's nothing?"

"Nothing," she said again, panic swelling in her chest like a balloon. She knew she was acting far from rational. If she kept it up, they'd wrestle it away from her and see what it was before she could. She couldn't have that - on the slim chance that it was from...

"I... I wrote a journal entry. It brought back some memories, so I tore it from my book and before I knew it... you two were in here." She gave a worried glance to the notebook on her nightstand that her parents had suggested she keep, hoping they wouldn't notice it had gone untouched since her arrival.

"Oh... oh, baby..." Her mother was already choking back sobs as she found frail, little arms wrap around her neck, fragile fingers lacing in her hair. Her mother shook with quiet sobs. Claudia felt no pity for her mother, nor her father who put his arm around the two women solemnly, she just wanted them out of her bedroom so she could inspect what it was in her hand before they could.

Maybe it wasn't a dream.

Maybe that all happened yesterday and for some reason, she didn't remember going to bed.

What was in her hand? What was it?

Despite her wishes, her own eyes brimmed with tears as her frustration and paranoia wracked her body. However, the act seemed to convince her parents that they were indeed helping her and after some minutes - or what felt like hours to Claudia - of holding and reassuring her, they finally left her room.

Claudia sat on her bed, staring back at the door as though they would rush back in and demand to read the entry that was supposedly in her hand, but they had already assured her before they wouldn't touch the notebook should she choose to use it.

She looked down at her hand, glancing back at her door frame every few seconds, until finally she opened her palm and unwrinkled the paper mess that had crumpled there.

Up back at her stared a woman with big doe eyes, beautiful wavy hair, and a clearly practiced smile. Claudia's stomach hurled into a pit as her mouth dried and her first excited feelings diminished within seconds.

Catherine.

Claudia was filled with disbelief. Even after burning up, the damn bitch was still haunting her. Immediately she was filled with anger, jealousy, and pain. They nearly died for this damn photo. For this damn Catherine.

He would have let them die for Catherine. Never for Claudia. Only Catherine.

What a mess he'd become.

What a mess *she'd* become.

Claudia wanted to call out to her parents, scream for them to console her - but before she could, she heard shattering come from what sounded to be the living room down the hallway. Before she could even try to investigate, her mother was in the room with her arms around her, her father passing her doorway with a gun in his hand, ready for an attack.

The girl felt the familiar rush of panic pumping through her blood as she waited to hear her father call out. The sound of her heartbeat echoed in her eardrums, and the picture of Catherine continued to burn in her palm. No, the hatred for this woman still stung very loudly in her brain, despite the dangers that were appearing before her family.

The woman would always haunt her. She would always be the proof that Claudia was second best - never what the doctor wanted. Never his companion, always his captive.

Nonetheless - she was his.

Claudia's head perked up immediately as the paper crinkled in her hand.

Who had put it there?

"Dad!" she found herself struggling away from her frail mother without her brain even functioning enough to tell her to move. "Dad - don't hurt him!" She was through the door and down the hallway faster than she'd managed to move since they brought her home. Her bare feet tingled at the cold of the hardwood hallway, bringing her closer and closer to what she hoped would be her savior.

"Dad!" She reached the living room, feet stopping instinctively at the sight of glass littering the floor. Her father stood by the hole that had once been their window, his back to her - stiff and sturdy.

"Don't... What happened?" She clutched the picture for dear life as though it was a lifeline. She knew she'd be punished for leaving creases in Catherine's pretty face, but how could she not hold so hard? It was all she had. It was the only hope that glimmered in her heart.

Who had put the picture in her hand?

"Calm down Claudia..." she heard her father breath. "Just... just calm down."

"I'm calm," she quipped. "Please don't hurt him...he...he isn't that bad -" In the distance the sound of a dog - or something that once was a dog - started howling.

Yes.

He'd come for her.

139

Finally, her father turned around, and she saw how pale the grown man had become. In his hands, Claudia could clearly see his rifle. He already held a finger at the trigger, ready to shoot whatever it was he'd just seen. If Claudia had been in her right mind, she'd wince considering the danger. However, her only thoughts were on her coming salvation.

Claudia then noticed what she had hoped her father hadn't; at his feet lay another crumpled piece of paper. She motioned to stride toward it.

"Don't," her father snarled. She stopped with a snap, and stood, waiting.

Her father glanced about the neighborhood suspiciously before reaching down to grab the paper. He glanced at it briefly, but only for a moment before she heard him make a guttural grunt in the bottom of his throat, and hoist the gun up again to point out of the broken window.

"This isn't funny!" he bellowed. "Who th'fuck did this?!" His voice cut the air like a knife. From behind Claudia, she could hear her mother calling, demanding to know what was going on, and if she should call the cops.

You mean they hadn't yet?

Claudia's heart raced in hope as she cautiously approached her father before snapping the paper out from between the gun and his hands.

"Claudia -stop it!" he immediately hissed as she crunched through the glass away from him, barely taking heed of the slicing pain that was shooting through her feet.

"Please!" she heard him plead as she ran out the front door and into the yard, trying to unwrinkle the paper to read what the contents were. From behind, she heard the dark thumps of her father coming after her, but she didn't mind. She'd make sure to outrun him - nothing would stop her now. But before she could react further she heard the sound of metal clashing with something heavy and her father grunting again before another thump hit the floor. She didn't need to turn around to know he'd been attacked. She knew he was on the ground already, that now, no one was chasing her.

She stopped to catch her breath. But instead of breathing - she laughed. She laughed as hard as her little body would allow it to until she was shaking with excitement. From behind her, she heard lighter footsteps approach. She only continued laughing as she felt a hand rest on her shoulder and a high pitched voice, one that sounded like nails on a chalkboard, whisper, "Read it."

So she did.

It was simple. One line. Scratched in the messiest of handwriting. But she recognized it. She'd seen it on countless notes strewn across the cabin's messy living room floor. All barely legible, all worse than chicken scratch. Anyone who had seen this handwriting in the past would immediately recognize it.

And what did it read?

It read: *Give me back what is mine.*

What is mine.

Claudia was finally his. Her heart soared.